"Has he already had what he wants?"

Mark's tone was angry. Lucy swung her hand up to hit his face, but he caught it in midair. "Well? Has he made love to you?" he persisted.

"It's none of your business!" Lucy snapped.

"Has he?"

"What do you think?" Lucy asked mockingly. "We found a nice secluded spot on the beach." She smiled. It seemed as though the words were coming out of their own volition. "We had...a lot of fun!" she finished, and gave him an impudent smile.

Mark let her go abruptly, and the contempt on his face seared her to the heart. "God, what a fool I've been!" he said savagely. "Thinking you were a little innocent who needed protection, while all the time—all the time...."

He turned away then, and Lucy watched as he slowly walked out of her life.

The Girl Between

by

SHEILA DOUGLAS

Harlequin Books

TORONTO • LONDON • LOS ANGELES • AMSTERDAM
SYDNEY • HAMBURG • PARIS • STOCKHOLM • ATHENS • TOKYO

Original hardcover edition published in 1980
by Mills & Boon Limited

ISBN 0-373-02392-8

Harlequin edition published March 1981

CHAPTER ONE

'IF you put that notice up,' said Caroline Grant, 'I shall stop coming home.'

She stood in the centre of the kitchen, her thin face flushed with anger. 'Well?' she asked belligerently. 'What about it?' and she thumped the offending notice, which was propped up on the old Welsh dresser.

Her sister Lucy looked at the piece of hardboard, painted by their brother William only last night. It had a white background and black lettering, painstakingly executed:

BED AND BREAKFAST OR FULL BOARD.
LONG OR SHORT STAYS.

'Sit down, Caroline,' Lucy suggested, 'and have some breakfast. More tea, William?'

William, who was only fourteen, was less tolerant than Lucy. 'So don't come home,' he muttered. 'We'll bear up.'

'William!' exclaimed Lucy, and Caroline glared at the boy.

'You little beast!' She rounded on her sister. 'It's your fault he's like this. You spoil him outrageously.' She dragged out a chair and sat down heavily, then pushed a cup in her sister's direction. 'I haven't time for a long argument. I'm due at the hospital by nine,' for Caroline was a house physician at Barnslow General Hospital and took her work very seriously.

Lucy poured tea for her sister and tried hard to be patient. 'There isn't really anything to argue about. We need the money and this is one way of making it.'

Caroline spooned sugar into her tea and stirred angrily. 'It's so—so degrading! Dad was a senior executive. We had a position in the neighbourhood. What will people say?'

'Does it matter what they say?' Lucy asked quietly. 'Lots of people are doing this sort of thing nowadays. We're lucky to have a big enough house.'

Caroline refused to be placated. 'It's so unnecessary. Dad may still get a job.'

'After two years?' Lucy murmured, thinking of the many many advertisements her father had answered, at first with hope and then with increasing lack of confidence. He had been made redundant when the engineering firm he worked for had been taken over by another organisation, a common enough story these days—a shattering blow to a man's pride and one from which her father had not yet recovered.

'Mother would never have allowed it if she'd been alive,' Caroline persisted doggedly, draining her tea and rising from the table. She pulled on her jacket and picked up her car keys. 'I meant what I said, Lucy! I shan't come here if you take lodgers.'

The door slammed behind her. 'Good riddance,' said William, and then doubtfully, 'Did she mean it?'

Caroline was inclined to exaggerate. She thrived on melodrama.

'I shouldn't think so,' Lucy rejoined, smiling at her young brother across the breakfast table. 'More toast? How many?'

'Two to start with.' William had a voracious appetite, though he remained rake-thin. 'What she said about Mother —do you think that was true?'

'I'm sure it wasn't. Mother was far too sensible. She wouldn't have liked strangers in her house, but she'd have put up with it because it's the obvious thing to do. That or sell it and move into a smaller place.'

Lucy sighed, remembering the near quarrel which had resulted when they had weighed up the alternatives. Her father, who had sunk into a disquieting apathy these days, had taken no active part in the argument. Caroline favoured selling and sixteen-year-old Susan agreed with Caroline, as she always did. William had been Lucy's only support.

Now he gobbled his toast down and rose to his feet. 'Let's fix it, then, Luce. See how it looks.'

He tucked the noticeboard under one arm, picked up the toolbox and made for the door. Ten minutes later the board was in place.

'It looks fine,' said Lucy, standing back from the gate-post where William had just screwed it.

Her brother looked doubtful. 'It's not absolutely straight. Perhaps I should take it off again.'

William was a perfectionist. Lucy smiled and shook her head. 'Don't fuss. It'll do. Now we just have to hope that someone turns up.'

'I'm sure they will. It's the right time of year and this is quite a busy road.'

Lucy wished she could share her brother's optimism, but if he was wrong and no one came then all the un-pleasantness would have been for nothing.

A thrush sang from the flowering cherry near the gate. Lucy took a deep breath of the early morning air. It was a glorious May day and the front garden looked its best, bright with tulips and grape hyacinths and the shrubs that had been planted by her mother, since she had first come to Marsh House as a young bride. When Lucy mourned her mother, dead for three years, she would tell herself that a beautiful garden was the best memorial anyone could have, a living reminder of the past, which was why she devoted so much time to tending it, and keeping it as lovely as it had been in her mother's day.

The house was worth looking at too—a mellow brick farmhouse, built in the reign of Queen Anne. A graceful house, large enough to accommodate at least six extra people, if they were lucky enough to attract anyone. 'I'm sure you're right, William,' said Lucy with a sudden spurt of confidence. 'A lot of cars pass here on their way to the coast.'

For the Grant family lived near Barnslow on the Welsh borders, and many holidaymakers heading for North Wales

chose to make a detour to avoid the crowded main roads.
Their house was on a B road, a mile outside the nearest
village and less than three miles from Barnslow. They
might have to wait a few days, but someone was bound
to come in the end.

William picked up a fallen Rawlplug and a box of screws,
and followed his sister up the garden path. 'Do you need
me for anything else, Luce?' When she shook her head he
looked relieved. 'Then I'll pop round to Don's place. We
thought we'd go on the river this morning.'

It was a Saturday, which was why he wasn't at school,
but he had never been one to lie in bed, unlike Susan who
could only be dragged out with difficulty. Lucy went back
into the kitchen and switched the kettle on. It was the
original old farmhouse kitchen, large and comfortable, and
although the Grants weren't farmers, they used it these
days more than any other room in the house. In the past,
when her father had been a top executive and entertained
a good deal, only the children had eaten in the kitchen
or done their studies there. Lucy thought what a good thing
it was that the dining-room and sitting-room had not been
much used in the last few years, so that they were still in
excellent condition. The visitors would eat and sit there
and watch colour television, while the family made do
with the old black and white set in the kitchen.

She made tea and took it upstairs. Her father had moved
out of the large front room that he had slept in through-
out his married life. He had chosen a small back room
with a view over the marsh towards the river.

Lucy went in and drew the curtains. He stirred and
muttered sleepily. 'Is it that late? I'm sorry.'

She put the small tray on his bed table and stooped to
kiss his forehead. 'There's no hurry, Dad. But it's such a
lovely day it would do you good to get into the garden.'

Her father was in his middle fifties, but looked ten years
older, with little trace left of the forceful and effective
businessman he had once been. There was a two-day

stubble on his chin, because sometimes he couldn't be bothered to shave. His colour was poor, for in bad weather he seldom went out, rising late and sitting huddled by the kitchen stove, drinking whisky that they could ill afford. Lucy worried about him increasingly and tried hard not to show it.

'The deed's done! We've put up the noticeboard.' She spoke lightly, hoping he would not react as violently as Caroline had done.

She need not have worried; he was too apathetic to care. 'Have you, Lucy? I don't suppose it'll do any good.' He propped himself up on one elbow and reached for his tea.

Lucy picked up the second cup and went back along the corridor to Susan's room. She drew the curtains on to teenage pin-ups and a wild scattering of clothes, that shocked her tidy nature. Susan had been to a party last night and had tried on just about everything in her wardrobe, grumbling as always that she hadn't a thing to wear. The profusion of clothes thrown over chair backs, on the end of the bed, lying on the floor, seemed to disprove this, though many of them were cast-offs from an older cousin, a fact which young Susan hated. Few of them were of really good quality, but Susan was so pretty that she looked good in the cheapest gear.

Lucy drew the sheet back from her sister's red-gold hair. 'Wake up, Sue! It's nine-thirty.'

Susan's face was flushed with sleep. She opened the dark brown eyes that were so striking with the red hair, and blinked crossly. 'So what? Go away, Lucy,' and she pulled the sheet over her head again.

'You asked me to wake you. Isn't Stephen coming at ten?'

Susan surfaced again and stretched out a smooth young arm for the teacup. In a flower-sprigged nightie, with her hair tumbled around her face, she looked deliciously pretty, a young girl for whom life was good, in spite of the decline in the family fortunes. The things that worried Lucy so much, making ends meet, her father's increasing dependence on alcohol, hardly touched Susan's consciousness, so totally was she absorbed in her own affairs.

'Has Caro gone?' she asked.

'Ages ago.'

'Was she in a better temper this morning?'

'Worse if anything. She said she wouldn't come home if I put that notice up.'

Susan lay back on the pillows, eyeing her sister through absurdly long lashes. 'But you did just the same?'

'Of course. And I meant what I said last night, Sue. If a lot of people come you'll have to move to one of the attic rooms.'

Susan's lip stuck out ominously.

'Only in an emergency,' Lucy added hastily, feeling that she couldn't face another sisterly display of temperament. 'It'll probably be weeks before you need to, if at all.'

Susan said sulkily, 'Caro's right—it's a rotten idea. We could have moved into a smaller house in Barnslow.'

'And what would we have lived on?'

'On what we made from selling this place.'

'And when that was gone? Oh, darling, don't you see, this is our only asset? When you and William are grown up then we might leave.' She rose from the end of the bed. 'The water's hot if you want a shower. You will tidy your room before you go out?'

Susan pulled a face and Lucy knew that she would leave the bedroom as it was. To assert her independence. To show that she was annoyed. Just to be difficult. There was some excuse for Susan, though, because she was only sixteen, and these were supposed to be the awkward years. Caroline, twenty-four and a qualified doctor, should have had the maturity to come to terms with their present situation.

Lucy sighed and went downstairs, going through in her mind all the jobs that still needed doing. She had vacuumed and polished the spare bedrooms until they sparkled with cleanness. She had stocked up the larder and baked a dozen pies, both sweet and savoury, which were now in the deep-freeze. That had been on the advice of Mrs Rudge, who lived down the road and had been taking in holiday visitors for years.

It had been Mrs Rudge who had first put the idea into Lucy's head. 'Why don't you make use of that huge house of yours, dearie? I can tell you, I would. You could make a small fortune.'

Hardly that, thought Lucy, but it would keep them going. They would be able to pay their bills. On an impulse she telephoned Mrs Rudge to say that this was the big day. 'We put the notice up this morning. I wonder how long we'll have to wait.'

'Not long if this fine weather holds,' Mrs Rudge said comfortably. 'I'm full for the weekend, so if anyone else calls I'll recommend you.'

She was as good as her word. Kind, dependable Mrs Rudge, who had cleaned for Lucy's mother many years ago, before she ran her own boarding house. She had known Lucy as a schoolgirl, and still on occasion treated her as one. Lucy put up with this gladly, however, because she valued Mrs Rudge's advice.

At three o'clock that afternoon the first visitors arrived, a married couple in their thirties with two children.

'We were recommended to come here,' the man said, eyeing the delightful garden and the charming old house. 'Nice place you've got, miss. You can take us?'

'Yes indeed!' exclaimed Lucy. 'Park your car in the yard over there. I'll get my brother to help with your cases.'

'No need,' said the man. 'We're travelling light,' but Lucy was away already to call William, who was stretched out on a rug on the back lawn, reading a magazine on model engineering.

The visitors were delighted with their rooms, and the

children were intrigued by the dark exposed beams and
the small-paned windows. 'They've never been in an old
house like this,' their mother explained. 'Is there any chance
of an evening meal at such short notice?'

'Yes, of course,' smiled Lucy, blessing Mrs Rudge for
urging her to stock up the freezer. 'Would steak and kidney
pie do? And perhaps a fruit salad? With fresh cream? We
get it from our local farm.'

'Sounds fine,' said the young woman, and wistfully, 'I
suppose we couldn't have a cup of tea?'

'Of course you can. Come down when you're ready,'

Lucy rushed off, full of enthusiasm and delighted with
her visitors. 'Such a nice family,' she told William, laying
a tray with tea things and emptying a packet of biscuits
on to a plate.

William helped himself to a couple and she slapped his
hand away. 'Calm down,' he implored. 'There's no need
to get so worked up!'

Lucy caught sight of herself in the small mirror above
the sink. She looked flushed and excited and rather untidy,
so she combed her hair quickly and washed her hands.

'And there's no need to go on so,' William added with
brotherly candour. 'You were positively gushing at them.
They're only people, after all.'

Lucy laughed a little selfconsciously, for William was a
stern critic of his elders. Had she talked too much? If so
it was entirely due to nerves, for she was usually a quiet
girl and seldom lost her composure. She was glad that her
father and Susan were out and that Caroline was on duty
this weekend. It was easier coping with no one else around
apart from William, who might be critical, but was most
definitely on her side.

The weekend visitors stayed until Monday, and Lucy was
pegging out their sheets when she saw a Post Office van
draw into the yard. Two young men got out and asked if
she had rooms to let.

'We're engineers, miss, working on that new telecom-

munications site near Barnslow. We'd want them for at
least a fortnight.'

Better and better, thought Lucy happily, showing them
the two single bedrooms at the back of the house. They
told her that Mrs Rudge had sent them over. They would
want breakfast and an evening meal, and if she could
manage it, packed lunches as well.

They were young and cheerful, and around Lucy's own
age, which was twenty-two. They said they would prefer
to eat in the kitchen, but mindful of the family, who were
not yet used to strangers in their midst, she said firmly that
visitors ate in the dining-room.

Susan was openly disapproving and had scarcely been
civil to the weekend visitors. Her father had grunted at
them and kept out of their way. What he would make of
these pleasant but rather brash young men, Lucy couldn't
imagine. Caroline, who had telephoned last night, was
unlikely to be home until the weekend, if then.

The Post Office engineers had been established for over a
week, and various overnight visitors had come and gone,
when Lucy had a telephone call from the assistant secretary of Barnslow General Hospital.

'I wonder if you could help one of our doctors, Miss
Grant? He's a new arrival and there's been a muddle over
his accommodation.'

'Put him up, you mean, Mr Brown? Yes, we do have
a room, but who told you about us?' It didn't seem likely
that Caroline would have done so.

Mr Brown explained that Sister Hart on Lister Ward
had mentioned Lucy's name. And Sister Hart, she knew,
was Mrs Rudge's sister-in-law.

'Is he on his own?' she asked. 'No family?'

'No, Miss Grant. He's unmarried. Mr Franklin, our
new consultant surgeon.'

Lucy felt a moment's unease. She had assumed it would
be a junior doctor. A consultant would be older, perhaps

more demanding. And what would Caroline say? Her sister was very conscious of her status as a professional woman. She would most certainly not like the idea of a senior colleague knowing that her family ran a boarding house.

'Um—Mr Brown—I think perhaps I'd better discuss it with my sister. It might be a bit embarrassing taking someone from the hospital.'

Lucy knew Mr Brown quite well and hoped he would understand. He was silent for a few moments and when he came on the line again he sounded cross. Cross and impatient. 'Oh, really, I did think you'd be more cooperative. I'm very busy, Miss Grant, and I've already spent a lot of time trying to sort this out.'

'Why can't Mr Franklin sort it out for himself?' Lucy enquired, quite reasonably, she thought, but Mr Brown made an exasperated sound.

He explained that when Mr Franklin was appointed consultant he had written to the hospital secretary, asking that accommodation should be found for him, until he could move into a place of his own. 'Unfortunately,' said Mr Brown, sighing heavily, 'no immediate action was taken —not my fault, I assure you—and by the time I was informed of Mr Franklin's requirements there wasn't a hotel room to be had. The Festival, you know.'

Barnslow was justifiably proud of its Arts Festival, which ran for three weeks. Lucy usually went to it, but this year she had been unable to afford it. She thought for a moment, then said a little uncertainly, 'I suppose we could take him for a fortnight, then he could move into a hotel when the Festival's over.'

'Thank you, my dear. That's a big load off my mind. He's been decidedly critical over this unfortunate business, and I've borne the brunt of it, because the secretary is on holiday.'

It was arranged that Mr Franklin should come round that evening. 'To see if the accommodation is suitable. I

wouldn't dare take it for him. He's inclined to be ...
choosy.'

For choosy read difficult, thought Lucy. 'Where is he
staying now?' she asked.

'In the residents' quarters, in a—ahem—in a house surgeon's room,' of which the choosy Mr Franklin would most
certainly not approve!

'If it's anything like my sister's room,' said Lucy with
some amusement, 'it's rather poky for a consultant.'

'Exactly,' agreed Mr Brown with feeling. 'I'm sure what
you have to offer will be much more attractive.' He asked
after her father then, who only a few years ago had been
chairman of the Hospital Management Committee.

Lucy fobbed him off with a noncommittal reply, and
when he had rung off went upstairs to look over the bedrooms. Her parents' old room was the nicest, spacious,
well decorated and with its own bathroom. Her mother's
bureau stood under the window and there was a comfortable armchair in one corner. Mr Franklin couldn't possibly have any objections. Would she have to feed him or
would he eat at the hospital? She had forgotten to ask.

She went downstairs again and out into the garden,
accompanied by their old spaniel, Beryl. Her father was
having his afternoon nap, and Susan and William were not
due back from school until five o'clock. That gave her at
least an hour to do some weeding, before she smartened
herself up for Mr Franklin's visit.

Half an hour later she was totally absorbed in her work,
with the afternoon sun beating down and the gentle drone
of bees in the ceanothus bush beside her. It was the hottest
day of the year. Beryl lay stretched out contentedly, snor-
ing gently. Lucy had already discarded her sweater and
was working in a T-shirt and jeans, with an old pair of
sneakers on her feet. She knelt at the edge of the lawn,
hand weeding a rose bed, happy and absorbed.

When footsteps sounded on the stone-flagged path she
didn't even turn her head, thinking it was her father, risen

from his nap. Then Beryl gave a low growl and she squinted into the sun.

'Excuse me,' a deep voice said. 'Can you tell me where Miss Grant is?'

'I'm Miss Grant.' She rose to her feet, pushing her hair back as she did so. A salesman? Someone asking for accommodation?

'Miss Lucy Grant,' the man said. 'Your sister, I suppose?'

He topped her by more than a head, an elegant, assured, bad-tempered looking man. 'Well?' he asked impatiently. 'Where is your sister?'

'I'm Lucy Grant, and you're——' she should have realised it before—'you're Mr Franklin. But you were supposed to be coming this evening.'

He looked her over from the crown of her head to the toes of her old sneakers, in what Lucy considered a most disagreeable way. She put up a hand selfconsciously to her hair, knowing it must be untidy.

'I was free unexpectedly early,' he said, stooping to pat Beryl. 'But Brown must have given me the wrong name. *You* can't run this place!'

'Why not?' asked Lucy coolly, wishing Beryl wouldn't fawn over him so sloppily.

He gave her another of those assessing looks. His eyes were grey and very penetrating, uncomfortably direct, missing nothing. 'I'll bet his house surgeons don't like him,' thought Lucy, shifting uneasily under that steady gaze.

'For heaven's sake!' he exclaimed in exasperation. 'You're just a young girl. I was expecting someone older—more experienced.'

'I'm twenty-two,' Lucy said, with an attempt at recovering her dignity. 'Quite old enough to be capable.'

Mr Franklin heaved a sigh and dug his hands into the pockets of his well cut jacket. 'I should have preferred a hotel, but the hospital staff have messed things up, so I'll have to take what's going.' He looked towards the house.

'This is a nice old place. I suppose it will do until I find something more suitable.'

'Patronising beast!' thought Lucy indignantly, as she led him through a side door into the hall.

At just that moment her father came downstairs, bleary-eyed from his sleep, tieless, unshaven. He shuffled past them with a muttered 'Afternoon!' and went out of the front door.

Mr Franklin stared after him with evident distaste. 'One of your visitors, Miss Grant?'

'My father,' Lucy said stiffly. 'The room's on the first floor,' and she climbed the stairs ahead of him.

Mr Franklin stood in the centre of her parents' old bedroom, surveying it critically, while Lucy wandered over to the windows. Catching sight of herself in the dressing table mirror, she gave a horrified gasp because she looked even worse than she had expected. She had rubbed earthy hands over her hot face while she was gardening, so that her nose and cheeks were streaked with dirt. Her T-shirt, fresh that morning, looked as if she had been wearing it for a week. No wonder Mr Franklin had not been impressed!

He came up behind her and she swung round from the mirror, tissue in hand, colouring hotly under his amused look. 'I didn't realise I was in quite such a mess.' She dabbed ineffectually at her dirty cheeks, smearing them further.

'Soap and water might be more effective,' he suggested. 'I'll take the room, Miss Grant, if the sitting-room's as good. And I must have a bathroom to myself.'

'The bathroom's through there.' Lucy opened the door on to it, a pretty blue and white room with an air of comfort and freshness, decorated during the last year of her mother's life. She hated the idea of this disagreeable man sleeping where her mother had once slept, but she couldn't afford to be sentimental. She shut the door again.

'The sitting-room is on the ground floor,' she told him.

'It has a nice view over the garden.'

'I should prefer one on this floor.'

'I'm afraid that's impossible. There are only bedrooms upstairs.'

He frowned, then pointed to the connecting door that led into another bedroom, empty at present. 'What's through there?' He opened it, glanced around, shut the door again. 'If you shift the beds out and move a few chairs in it would do. I must have a sitting-room.'

Annoyed by his peremptory manner, Lucy pointed out that the other guests were quite satisfied with the sitting-room downstairs.

'The other guests?' He looked disgusted. 'You don't expect me to share a sitting-room, Miss Grant? I can't possibly do that.'

'You could sit in your bedroom if you found their company that disagreeable,' Lucy said tartly, then blushed under his withering look.

'And entertain my visitors there? I want a second room, Miss Grant, or I shall have to ask Brown to find me something else. Though the man's such a fool he'll take another week over it.'

Lucy would dearly have liked to tell him to do just that, but a moment's reflection made her change her mind. If Mr Franklin rented two rooms he would have to pay for two rooms, but she would only have to cook and clean for one person. She would have less work to do, and although she was managing better than she had expected, overnight visitors meant more work than someone who stayed for a fortnight.

'All right, Mr Franklin,' she said slowly. 'You can have the two rooms, though you do realise both bedrooms are double ones, so you'll have to pay accordingly?'

'Of course,' he said carelessly, as one to whom money was unimportant.

Lucy preferred the families who asked a shade anxiously

what her terms were. 'Will you be eating at the hospital?'
she asked.

'I shall have lunch there, but I shall want an evening
meal. And breakfast at a quarter to eight. All right?'

'I suppose so. Most of our visitors eat at eight-thirty,'
though she did serve the Post Office engineers at eight-
fifteen.

'A quarter to eight,' he said firmly. 'I like to be early at
the hospital. I hope you have a good cook.'

Lucy could feel her colour rising. 'I do the cooking. No
one has complained so far.' In fact she enjoyed cooking and
had had plenty of practice since her mother became ill.

Mr Franklin registered surprise and faint amusement.
'You do have some help, Miss Grant?' Or how can you
manage? his tone implied.

'The family lend a hand,' Lucy said quickly. Not as
often as she would have liked, unfortunately, for they were
none of them keen on domestic work. 'When I'm properly
established I shall engage someone to help me,' she added,
then wished that she hadn't.

'When you're ...' Mr Franklin pinned her with that
disconcerting gaze. 'How long have you been running a
boarding-house, Miss Grant?'

Lucy stared back at him, furious with herself for blushing so easily. She swallowed and spoke the truth, because
she was an honest girl. 'For—for about ten days, actually.
But you needn't worry, I'm perfectly competent. I've been
running this house for years, ever since my mother died in
fact——' She caught herself up, aware that she was babbling, but this man made her unaccountably nervous, 'Anyway,' she finished flatly, 'you can always leave if you don't
like it, can't you?'

'Quite right,' he agreed briskly, and headed for the
stairs. They went out into the yard, where a gleaming blue
M.G. was parked. Just the sort of car he would have!
William would certainly admire it.

'You'll be coming tomorrow?' asked Lucy.

'I should prefer to move in tonight. My quarters at the hospital are very inadequate. All right, Miss Grant?' He patted Beryl, who had followed them everywhere, swung himself into the low seat of the M.G. and reached for the ignition key.

Lucy frowned. 'The sitting-room won't be ready. I shall need some help to move the furniture.'

He waved a large, well kept hand. 'Tomorrow will do for that. I'm a reasonable man, Miss Grant. Expect me back by nine.'

When she had watched the M.G. turn out of the yard, Lucy took a deep steadying breath and made her way back into the house. Mr Franklin wasn't going to be an easy man to have around. He might claim to be reasonable, but Lucy felt sure that he would be difficult and demanding. Hard to please and slow to praise—the sort of man she had never cared for. Too sure of himself, and too successful too young, for surely most consultants were older when they were first appointed? This man looked no more than in the early thirties. She must ask Caroline about him. Meanwhile she had to start preparing supper for the young Post Office engineers, whose appetites were even larger than William's.

CHAPTER TWO

Lucy decided to rearrange Mr Franklin's room that evening, before he returned. She would have no one to help by day except her father, who wasn't fit to lug heavy furniture about. She and William could move the light stuff, and if she asked them nicely the Post Office men would help with the beds.

'Course we'll help,' smiled Brian, the breezy extrovert one. 'Any time, love. You've only to ask.'

They were willing but inexpert, and Lucy winced as they banged and scraped the two single beds upstairs to an attic.

'The wardrobe too?' asked Harry, the quiet one.

'I shouldn't bother,' said Lucy, but Brian disagreed.

'A wardrobe's not the thing in a living-room. No trouble, love, none at all.'

They were sturdy young men and they manhandled the wardrobe up the stairs with no ill effect to themselves, but with some damage to the wallpaper. Lucy wondered if the room looked too bare now. She and William brought the big easy chair through from the front bedroom, then her mother's little inlaid bureau.

'Another chair,' she mused. 'A table perhaps. Yes, and a hearthrug.'

'I'll get the chair,' offered Brian, bounding into the room, plump and good-natured, perspiring from his exertions. William and Harry, having fetched the other things, departed.

'Where do you want the chair?' asked Brian, and Lucy pointed.

'By the fire, I think, don't you?'

He pushed it into place and she gave him a warm smile. 'I can't thank you enough for helping. You've been so kind.'

'Pleased to be of service,' he responded, his amiable face split by a grin. 'How about thanking me properly, then?' and he advanced on her purposefully.

For a moment Lucy didn't get his meaning, then she backed precipitately. Brian was a good-natured wolf; she had spotted that immediately from the assessing way he stared at her, and the loaded remarks he sometimes made. He came on grinning and caught her by the arms.

'Just a few kisses, love. I've fancied you since the first day. Harry likes your little sister, but I don't go for red-heads,' and he ran a hand down Lucy's long brown hair.

Short of an outright snub there was no way of avoiding him, and he had been very helpful. She submitted with as good a grace as she could, but as his kiss deepened and his arms tightened she began to struggle. Twisting her head away, she fought for breath.

'Brian, please—let me go!'

He smiled into her eyes, well pleased with himself. 'You're a doll, you really are,' and at that moment the door, which Brian had shut, began to open.

Lucy gave him a shove, stepped back quickly, tripped on the hearthrug and collapsed into the big armchair. As she righted herself she saw to her dismay that Mr Franklin had arrived, a suitcase in either hand.

The look on his face told her quite plainly that he knew exactly what they had been doing. He dumped his case and glanced around.

'Looks fine, Miss Grant. I didn't expect such prompt action.' His gaze shifted to Brian, taking in his gaudy shirt, skin-tight jeans and tan ankle boots.

Brian grinned back at him. 'I'm the man for action! In more ways than one! There's a programme I want to watch.' He raised a hand in airy farewell and left them raising a low growl from Beryl as he passed the old dog.

Beryl was choosy about people, which made it all the more irritating that she seemed to have taken a great fancy to the objectionable Mr Franklin. He had looked so contemptuous when he first came into the room, and Lucy had been determined to eradicate the afternoon's bad impression at their next meeting. She had changed out of her scruffy gardening clothes into a neat denim skirt and a pretty blue blouse. She had wanted to impress him as cool and efficient, and instead he had found her in his room being kissed by Brian. Lucy was no snob, but Brian wasn't the sort of young man with whom she cared to be associated. She wanted to explain this to Mr Franklin, but couldn't think how to put it.

The surgeon looked impatient, as if he wanted to get rid of her. 'I'll see you in the morning, Miss Grant. I like a cooked breakfast. And coffee. All right?'

'Bacon and eggs? That sort of thing?' Lucy murmured, moving towards the door, and then on a sudden impulse, 'Brian was helping us shift the furniture. He's a bit ... brash, and ... and ... you know ...' Under his cool gaze she stumbled on. 'He ... he thought I owed him a few kisses in return.'

Mr Franklin picked up one of his cases and put it on the table. 'Really, Miss Grant?' He sounded bored and supercilious.

Lucy glared at his bent head. 'Goodnight, Mr Franklin. Oh, come *on*, Beryl! Leave the man alone.' Even to her own ears her voice was waspish and disagreeable, and she shut the door on him with ill-concealed relief.

Caroline telephoned around ten o'clock, when the family were gathered in the kitchen having hot drinks. Although she still disapproved she seemed to have come to terms with the changes at home.

'How's it going?' she asked Lucy. 'You must be working awfully hard for very little profit.'

'I'm sure there are easier ways of earning money,' Lucy

agreed equably, 'but I don't happen to be trained for any of them.'

There was a little pause. 'You make me feel very guilty, Lucy. Do you still mind terribly about giving up your music?'

'Not as much as I did,' said Lucy. 'Don't feel guilty, Caro. There wasn't much alternative. I was always more domesticated than you.'

'And more unselfish,' Caroline added wryly. 'Do you think some day you might be able to take it up again— when Susan and William are grown up?'

'Perhaps,' Lucy said with a casualness she didn't feel. The London college of music she had been attending when her mother became ill didn't award its places lightly. The Dean had been furious with her when she left after only one term, telling her that she was throwing away the chance of a fine career, that she had a real talent, that her teachers expected great things of her. That surely her family could manage without her? No one was indispensable.

Lucy had listened to him, and replied sadly that she had no alternative but to leave, that she must put her family before her career. William had only been eleven and Susan thirteen, bad ages to lose a mother, for they knew already that there was no hope. Her father, sunk in despair when he was told the news, had no resources with which to comfort his younger children, and Caroline had been about to start her final year at medical school.

'I thought I might come home tomorrow,' said Caroline, breaking into these thoughts of the past, an olive branch which Lucy was quick to accept.

'Oh, good,' and then she remembered their new lodger. 'Caro, have you met the new consultant surgeon, Mr Franklin?'

'Mark Franklin!' exclaimed Caroline. 'Of course I have. Why?'

'He's staying here for a week or two. Mr Brown rang

from the hospital and asked me to take him——'

'Lucy, honestly!'

'As a great favour. Because they messed up his accommodation.'

'You didn't have to agree,' Caroline snapped, sounding very upset. 'You know how I feel about taking anyone, but hospital staff, it's the absolute end! And Mark of all men! How could you?'

'You sound as if you know him quite well.'

'Of course I know him,' Caroline said edgily. 'He was my registrar at Q.C.H. when I did my surgery firm. He'll think it very odd that my sister runs a boarding house.'

Having met the superior Mr Franklin, Lucy thought that Caroline was probably right, but there wasn't much she could do about it now, and she felt that her sister, as so often, was overreacting. 'I expect you'd like to speak to Susan,' she suggested. 'See you tomorrow, then.'

'Possibly,' Caroline said coldly, and Lucy handed over to her younger sister.

Her father, hunched in his favourite chair by the stove, had shown no interest in the conversation. Caroline and he were not close. They hardly talked to each other these days.

William asked under his breath what Caroline had been on about. 'She sounded cross. She quacks so on the phone.'

Lucy laughed. 'She's upset about Mr Franklin. She seems to know him quite well.'

William drained his mug of Ovaltine. 'I wish she'd stayed in London. I thought she was going to do another job at Queen's College Hospital.'

'So did I, but for some reason she changed her mind.'

Lucy had been puzzled by Caroline's decision to take a job at Barnslow. Her sister was clever and ambitious, and to hear her talk in her student days the only place worth working in was London, and the absolutely top hospital was Queen's. Perhaps she had been motivated by a desire to help her family, though Lucy found this difficult to believe. Since she had qualified Caroline had given financial aid when things were really difficult, but she had always put her own affairs first. She was fond enough of them, but her fondness didn't extend to putting herself out on their account.

'I'm going to bed,' William announced. 'I wonder if Mr Franklin would give me a lift in that super car of his tomorrow.'

'You are not to ask him,' said Lucy to his departing back. 'What's wrong with the bus?'

He turned at the door and gave his quick, disarming grin. 'Nothing, except it's not an M.G.!'

After Susan had gone as well Lucy drew up a chair beside her father's. 'Darling Daddy, I know you must hate people in the house as much as Caroline does, but thanks for not being disagreeable about it.'

He shrugged defeatedly. 'I haven't much right to be disagreeable. Since I can no longer support my family I should be glad that you can.'

Self-pity and bitterness were destroying her father's character. Lucy knew that he had had a raw deal, but longed for him to adopt a more positive attitude to life. He had many friends in the district, but seemed to be cutting himself off from them all. Only the oldest and the most determined, like the rector and their local G.P., refused to be dismissed.

Next morning Lucy jumped out of bed at the first peal of her alarm clock. In the kitchen she laid rashers of bacon in the frying pan, cracked an egg, sliced tomatoes, then set about preparing Susan's sandwiches. William, thank goodness, ate the school meals, but Susan, who was finicky, refused to touch them. Such a pity that Mr Franklin insisted on eating earlier than the other visitors. Until now Lucy had been able to feed her brother and sister before the main morning rush.

She had set the dining-room table last night to save

time. Now she listened with only half an ear to the 'Today'
programme, because she was edgy about Mr Franklin's
breakfast. If she put it on too soon the bacon would be
spoilt. If she left it too late he would grumble because it
wasn't ready.

'Morning, Luce.' That was William, who always came
down before Susan. 'Isn't my breakfast ready yet?'

'I thought you and Mr Franklin could have it together.'

'In here?'

'No, silly. But at the same time, to save cooking twice.'
She turned on the ring beneath the frying pan, flicked down
the switch on the electric kettle and set the coffee per-
colating.

'I wouldn't mind coffee,' said William.

'You can jolly well have tea!'

'Why are you so snappy this morning?' Her brother
plonked himself down at the kitchen table and stared at
her. 'And sort of flustered too.'

'I am not flustered,' Lucy said crossly, and wished that
it was true. It was absurd to allow Mr Franklin to get
her so worked up. He was only another visitor, and she had
been coping quite adequately before he came.

She kept the connecting door to the dining-room open,
and as soon as he appeared started dishing up. 'Good
morning, Mr Franklin,' she said politely, placing his bacon
and eggs on the table.

He came over from the window, looking, she was relieved to see, quite agreeable. 'Good morning, Miss Grant.
I'm ready for that!'

He was a lot taller than she was, and well built. His
thick dark hair was slightly damp, his newly shaven skin
lightly tanned. He was, she admitted reluctantly, a very
attractive man, which made it rather surprising that he had
reached the rank of consultant without getting married.
These days most doctors married young, many while they
were still students.

'Coffee and toast will be through in a moment,' Lucy

said as he sat down. 'And if you want anything more, please ring the bell.'

She snatched a cup of tea and a slice of toast, urged Susan to get a move on and looked in again on Mr Franklin.

'That was fine,' he said pleasantly. 'What time is your evening meal, Miss Grant?'

'Seven o'clock. I hope you can manage that,' said Lucy with a touch of belligerence.

He caught the sound of it and gave her an amused look. 'No meal if I'm not on time? I'll do my best, Miss Grant.'

She had decided that it would be easier if he knew about Caroline before he bumped into her in the house. 'By the way'—she was carefully casual—'I believe you know my sister Caroline. She works at Barnslow General.'

'Good heavens, is Caroline Grant your sister?' He looked surprised. 'We were both at Queen's too. Bright girl. She'll go far,' and he was off, tucking his brief case under his arm.

William dashed to the kitchen window to watch the M.G. depart. 'Blow! I was going to ask him for a lift. I'm sure he wouldn't have minded.'

Susan, combing her long red hair for a second time at the mirror over the sink, told William not to make a nuisance of himself. 'Wait till you're asked, Billy, but it is a super car.'

Lucy half expected Caroline not to turn up that evening, but she arrived shortly after eight and noticeably on edge. The family were still at the supper table, but Caroline said she had already eaten. She smoked two cigarettes in quick succession, then asked where the visitors parked their cars.

'In the barn,' said Lucy. 'It's quite suitable since William and I cleared it out.'

'Mark too? Couldn't you let him have the garage?'

'I suppose he can have it if he objects to the barn.'

Caroline stubbed out a freshly lit cigarette and wandered

to the door. 'I think I'll look round the garden. It's a lovely evening and I've been indoors all day.'

As Lucy dumped the dishes in the sink her sister came round the side of the house, went into the barn and came out again. A few minutes later she returned to the kitchen. The others were grouped around the television at the far end of the big room. Caroline sat at the table and watched Lucy start on the dishes.

After a little desultory conversation she asked, 'What do you think of Mark?'

Lucy turned to look at her sister, whose normally pale skin had flushed slightly. She had an uneasy suspicion that the cause of Caroline's edginess was not the one she had at first assumed. Caroline might not like a colleague staying in their house, but it was more personal than that. She was interested in Mark Franklin. She had gone to the barn to see if he was in, which in fact he was not.

'I haven't exactly taken to him,' Lucy said wryly. 'But I expect he improves on acquaintance.'

Caroline gave a brittle laugh. 'Oh, he does! He most certainly does! You ask any one of a hundred females at Q.C.H.' She lit a fresh cigarette. 'Mark was just about the most sought-after man in the medical school.'

Lucy went on with the dishes. 'That explains the lordly manner, then. He's thoroughly spoilt by all that feminine adulation. What fools women are, Caro! Is he clever as well as good-looking?'

'Brilliant,' Caroline said fervently, and went into elaborate detail on the subject. Mark was unusually well qualified, a superb teacher, a technically accomplished surgeon, an excellent clinician. The list seemed endless and Lucy began to get bored by this paean of praise to a man she didn't even like.

When she could get a word in she observed quietly that he sounded too good to be true. 'I think he's rather disagreeable—arrogant too—and probably conceited.'

Caroline denied this vehemently. 'Though he has every

reason to be. He was easily the most outstanding man of his year. Everyone thought he was a sure thing for the next consultant post at Queen's, when he came back from the States.'

'But he didn't get it?'

'He didn't wait for it. He took this job at Barnslow.' Caroline frowned over this. 'Funny really. I wish a house job in surgery had been vacant instead of one in medicine.'

This remark confirmed Lucy's suspicions. She finished the pans and came to sit by her sister. The others were immersed in a T.V. thriller and the sound was enough to drown her next words . 'You ... fancy him, don't you, Caro?'

Caroline met her sister's eyes squarely. She nodded. 'I'm mad about him,' she admitted frankly. 'Have been for years. I've held my breath every time he's so much as looked at another girl, but so far he's unattached.'

Another thought struck Lucy. 'You took the job at Barnslow when you knew he was coming here, didn't you?'

Caroline nodded again. 'Yes. I nearly missed it, because I only heard of his appointment quite late. I was terrified I wouldn't get it. Those six months he was in the States were the longest six months of my life.'

Caroline was always inclined to dramatise, but the intensity of her feeling and the glitter in her eyes alarmed Lucy. Her sister appeared obsessed by Mark Franklin.

'If I'd realised how things were,' said Lucy worriedly, 'of course I wouldn't have taken him. I'm truly sorry, Caro.'

Caroline smiled. 'Don't be. As a matter of fact once I'd got over the shock I realised that it was a very good thing. I was delighted when I heard he was going to live in our mess, but I didn't see much of him except at meals. Here we're bound to meet more often.'

'We don't really have that much to do with the visitors,' Lucy pointed out, but Caroline disagreed.

'You may not—I'm different. I've worked with him. I've

been out with him a couple of times.'

'I hope you won't make it too obvious. Men hate being chased, Caro.'

Her sister looked offended. 'I'm not a complete fool. He hasn't a clue how I feel about him. Know where he went tonight?'

'No idea. I gave him a door key so that he can come in when he likes.'

Caroline usually left by ten, saying she needed to turn in early when she was off duty. Tonight she hung on until nearly midnight, though she looked worn out. When Lucy could scarcely keep her own eyes open, she said that she really must go to bed. She had to be up by a quarter to seven.

'All right,' sighed Caroline, and rose, looking disappointed and unhappy.

Lucy walked out with her sister, and as Caroline got into her Mini she said gently, 'There'll be other times. He'll be here for a fortnight.'

Caroline wound down the window. 'I know. I suppose you think I'm a complete fool, falling in love with a man who's never shown any interest in me?'

'But you said he'd taken you out.'

Caroline's face twisted and she gave a deprecating laugh. 'I was embroidering a bit. It was just a group thing. Do you think I'm a fool?'

'Of course I don't. It happens, doesn't it?' Once, years ago at her college of music, Lucy had been half in love with a fellow student, but she hadn't been obsessed with him as Caroline appeared to be with Mark. Perhaps it hadn't been love at all, for it hadn't survived their separation. Since then she had been too busy running the house and looking after the family to see much of any man.

Caroline smiled up at her. 'You've been great, Lucy. I really mean it. It's helped to let off steam to someone sympathetic.'

The sisters had different interests and were poles apart

in temperament, but they were sisters. The family ties were
strong. Lucy stayed awake longer than she usually did,
thinking about Caroline's affairs, and worrying in case she
should be hurt. A man as prosperous and successful as
Mark Franklin appeared to be would have a wide choice
of women. When—if—he decided to marry there was no
reason why it should be Caroline.

She was half asleep when she heard a car draw into the
courtyard, and a minute or two later a door closed softly
downstairs. The other visitors were all in, so it must be
Mark, returning at two in the morning. From work or
play? Lucy wondered, punched her pillow into shape and
drifted off to sleep.

Caroline had the weekend off and elected to spend it at
home, cancelling her intended trip to London. She arrived
just before ten on Friday night, coming into the kitchen
with a broad smile. If she had parked her Mini in the
barn she must have seen Mark's car, so she knew he was
in the house.

Lucy was just making hot drinks for the family. 'Oh,
good,' said Caroline, helping herself to biscuits. 'Does Mark
come down for a snack?' she asked casually.

'Good heavens no!' Lucy gave her sister a wry smile.
'He doesn't mix with the plebs!'

'You've never asked him to,' William pointed out.

Nor was she likely to, thought Lucy. Her attitude to
Mark Franklin hadn't changed. She had taken a dislike
to him at their first meeting, and although he was always
polite enough and moderately appreciative of her efforts,
she never felt at ease with him. He was, quite simply,
not her type.

'I shall ask him down!' exclaimed Caroline, jumping up
and making for the door.

'He won't want to come,' Lucy objected, but Caroline
was already running upstairs.

She was back a minute or two later, accompanied by

Mark, who was casually dressed in a sweater and slacks. He smiled at Lucy and in spite of herself she was jolted by the attraction of that smile, the first he had ever given her. Thick dark hair and clear grey eyes in a tanned face— there was no denying his physical appeal. It was his force- ful personality that she found hard to take.

'I could have sent you up a drink, Mr Franklin,' she said. 'Perhaps you'd have preferred that?'

He propped himself against the dresser and smiled at her again. 'I've been on my own all evening, Miss Grant.'

'If you're lonely you can come down to the kitchen any time you like,' said William. This remark surprised Lucy, for William was usually a reserved boy.

'Mr Franklin prefers his own sitting-room,' she said quickly.

The grey eyes were amused now, as if he knew how she felt about him. 'I thought you believed in fraternising with the lodgers, Miss Grant.'

He was referring to the incident with Brian, of course. Lucy blushed and was furious with herself for doing so. 'What do you want, Mr Franklin?' she snapped, and the others stared at her in surprise. 'Ovaltine or chocolate?' she added in a more agreeable tone.

'Chocolate, please, Miss Grant.'

'You do sound formal,' observed Caroline, who was look- ing animated now and almost pretty. 'My sister's name is Lucy.'

'I know.' The surgeon sat down beside Mr Grant, with whom he had never exchanged more than a few words. 'I hope you don't mind my joining you?'

He had nice manners when he chose, Lucy conceded, especially when her father gave so little in return. The older man muttered something and lowered his head over his mug. Caroline threw him an irritated look and started to talk medical shop. About Q.C.H., about Barnslow General, about mutual acquaintances of hers and Mark's.

When their father shambled out of the room with a

subdued 'Goodnight' to no one in particular, Mark asked quietly, 'Has he been ill?'

'You'd think so, wouldn't you,' Caroline snapped. 'No, it's just his way.'

Mark looked surprised, so Lucy felt obliged to explain. 'He still mourns our mother. And he lost his job the year after she died. I think the two blows were just more than he could take, and he's never recovered from them.'

Caroline looked disgusted. 'Mark isn't interested in Dad's problems,' but Mark refuted this firmly.

'Why shouldn't I be interested?' He looked at Lucy while he spoke, not at Caroline. 'If he had had your mother's support he might have coped better with being unemployed. Is there no hope of another job?'

Lucy shook her head sadly. 'Would you employ him as he is now? I wish you could have known him in the old days,' and her eyes went to a photograph on the kitchen dresser. Her father and mother stood, surrounded by their family, Caroline and Lucy at twelve and eleven, the little ones in front of them, looking very angelic.

Mark studied it thoughtfully. 'He certainly has changed. And so have you, Lucy! Pigtails and a brace on your teeth!' He was smiling as he looked at her.

He was being surprisingly nice about her father, sympathetic and understanding. Lucy wondered if she had judged him too hastily.

'Family photographs are the absolute end,' Caroline remarked. 'All that nostalgia for the past.'

'Sorry, Mr Franklin,' said Lucy, 'I didn't mean to bore you.'

'Mark,' he suggested. 'And you weren't boring me, my dear girl. Caroline has the wrong idea about some things.'

This mild reproof brought a tinge of colour to Caroline's cheeks. She busied herself with collecting the mugs and rinsing them. William and Susan went to bed, but Mark lingered, chatting to the two older girls.

When he finally left Caroline took a deep breath and expelled it slowly, stretching out in the old armchair. 'I hope he's not going away this weekend. Has he said anything to you?'

'No, he hasn't, so he's probably staying.' The Post Office engineers went home for weekends, so Mark would be the only visitor.

'He could eat with us,' suggested Caroline. 'It's silly giving him meals on his own.'

'He prefers it that way,' Lucy said quickly.

Caroline jumped up, dismissing this with a wave of her hand. 'How do you know? I shall ask him tomorrow. He can hardly refuse, and why should he want to?'

'Because he made it very plain the first day he came that he didn't want to mix with the other visitors. And if he's too grand for them he'll hardly want to muck in with us.' Mark's attitude about the sitting-room still rankled in Lucy's mind.

Caroline gave her a pitying look. 'That was before he realised who we were, idiot! I mean, we're not the sort of people who usually run a boarding house.'

'You're a snob, Caro,' said Lucy, and Caroline laughed, unusually good-humoured.

'So you keep saying. But I know I'm right. Look how friendly he was tonight.'

All the more reason not to presume that they were now on a different footing. That way embarrassment could lie. It was better to keep things on a strictly businesslike basis. And if Caroline refused to see that, it was because she was too besotted by Mark to think clearly. On these thoughts, which she kept to herself, Lucy said 'Goodnight' and went to bed. The morning would be time enough to try and make her sister see reason.

In the morning, however, there was no need. Mark drove off immediately after breakfast, returning very late at night. After lunch Caroline brought out a lounger and stretched out in the garden, glum and inconsolable, while Lucy got to work on the vegetable patch.

On Sunday morning she found a note on the kitchen table: 'Would appreciate sleeping in if it's all right with you. I'll skip breakfast, Mark.'

She had been asleep by the time he came in last night and she wondered where he had been. With a girl? Poor Caroline, if that was why he stayed out so late. The week-end was slipping by and her sister had barely seen him.

Lucy was rolling pastry for an apple pie when Mark finally appeared. 'Good morning. Apologies for coming down so late.'

'That's all right. Would you like a cup of coffee?'

'Love one.' He seated himself at the kitchen table and Lucy gave him a doubtful look. She was new to this business, but her thoughts last night had clarified one thing in her mind. It was a mistake to treat people who paid as one of the family. Especially Mark, who would probably have been staying at the best hotel in Barnslow if the hospital secretary hadn't been incompetent.

'I'm being a nuisance,' he said. 'Don't bother with the coffee.'

'It's not that. Wouldn't you prefer it in the dining-room?'

'My dear girl, what's wrong with the kitchen? Unless I'm in your way?'

She spooned instant coffee into a cup, added boiling water and passed it to him. 'I feel we're presuming on Caroline's acquaintance with you. I mean,' she mumbled, head in the refrigerator as she reached for the milk, 'this is a business arrangement, after all. Or it should be.' She poured the top of the milk into a small jug and placed it on the table, her face flushed.

Mark stared at her, then spooned sugar into his coffee, taking his time about replying. 'I can see that this set-up isn't easy for you. It's a new venture and you're still a bit out of your depth. No, let me finish——' He held up a hand when she tried to interrupt. 'But I'm your sister's colleague, so that puts me on a different footing. Well, doesn't it?' he ended with the smile that so transformed him.

Lucy dusted her hands with flour and went back to her pastry making. 'I suppose so,' she agreed with a little sigh. 'Will you be out again today?'

When he said that he wouldn't she asked if he wanted lunch. Mark nodded. 'And I'd rather not eat in splendid isolation! So may I join the family, Miss Grant?'

There was a gleam in his eyes that flustered Lucy, so that she bent over the worktop and gave all her attention to fluting the edge of the pastry. 'If you want to,' she murmured, and was further confused by his next remark.

'You don't approve of me, do you? I wish I knew why.'

The colour deepened in Lucy's cheeks. 'I hardly know you,' she managed to say. She shot a quick look at him and was annoyed by his air of relaxed amusement. He was so much more sophisticated than she was. He made her feel gauche and unsure of herself.

'And that's not a proper answer,' Mark returned, finishing his coffee and crossing over to her side. 'I'm looking forward to sampling some of that apple pie! You're a good cook, young Lucy. Perhaps I shan't move to a hotel after all.'

He made a joke of it, so that it didn't sound condescending, but Lucy wasn't at all sure that she wanted him to stay. He was no trouble to look after and less critical than she had expected him to be, but she never felt quite at ease with him, and there was still the problem of Caroline.

The longer Mark stayed on, the harder it would be for her sister when he left. There was no future in it for Caroline; Lucy was absolutely sure of that. Mark was hardly aware of her sister as a woman, and Caroline was deluding herself if she thought otherwise.

CHAPTER THREE

THE family were all on their best behaviour because of Mark's presence at lunch. They ate in the dining-room and Lucy felt that it was almost like the old days. Even her father had smartened himself up, to the extent of putting on a tweed jacket instead of the worn old pullover he practically lived in. William had brushed his shock of red hair and was refraining from the usual mealtime arguments with Susan, which irritated Caroline so much.

The spring lamb was tender. The greens and the mint were out of the garden. The cream was from their local farmer. Mark, who must have been hungry since he had had no breakfast, accepted a second helping of apple pie.

'Absolutely delicious,' he smiled. 'I've eaten so much I shan't want to go out this afternoon.'

'Do you have to?' asked Caroline. 'Why not sit in the garden and read the papers? It's a perfect day for loafing.'

'It is indeed,' agreed Mark. 'But I have to go over to our new house. I promised my fiancée I'd measure the windows, so she can start thinking about curtains.'

In the silence that followed this speech Lucy dared not look at Caroline, who was sitting on Mark's far side. She tried vainly to think of something to say, when William, bless him, jumped into the gap.

'I didn't know you had a house. Where is it? When are you moving in?'

'Not for months unless the builders get a move on,' Mark answered. 'Like to come with me this afternoon and have a look around? It's a nice old place. And you can help with the measuring.'

William looked delighted. 'Great! I've been longing for a ride in your M.G.'

Mark smiled. 'You should have asked me before,' he said pleasantly.

During this exchange Lucy cleared away the sweet plates and fetched the coffee. Mark went on talking, telling them about the house, which was in a village on the other side of Barnslow. He didn't say where his fiancée lived or when they were getting married. Caroline kept her head down, staring intently at her place mat, her face taut. She drank her coffee quickly and excused herself.

'What's biting Caro?' asked William.

Lucy pretended she hadn't heard and put a question of her own. 'You wouldn't have preferred a house in Barnslow, Mark? Closer to your work?'

He shrugged. 'It's only a mile or so outside town. Nearer than this place. Coming, William?'

Lucy washed the dishes and Susan dried them. She only half listened to her sister's chatter, until a remark that nearly made her drop a coffee cup.

'Isn't Mark absolutely dreamy? No wonder Caro's got a thing about him.'

'Rubbish!' said Lucy, briskly and dishonestly. 'You read too many silly romances, that's your trouble.'

'Caro's potty about him,' Susan persisted. 'Didn't you see her face at lunchtime?'

'Oh, go away, Susan!' Lucy exclaimed crossly.

Her young sister grinned and made for the door. 'I'm playing tennis with Stephen again. I don't expect I'll be back for tea.'

'Susan!' The girl poked her pretty face round the door enquiringly. 'Don't you dare repeat those silly remarks to anyone else! Don't you dare!'

'O.K., O.K.' The door shut noisily. Lucy went on tidying up, while she wondered if she should go and look for Caroline. In the end she decided against it and continued with yesterday's gardening. At four o'clock Caroline appeared, very pale and pink around the eyes, but quite composed.

'I think I'll look up Helen Goodwin,' she announced. 'I haven't seen her for ages!'

Helen lived about five miles away and had been to the same school as Caroline.

'Good idea,' said Lucy, dropping a runner bean into the shallow trench she had prepared. 'Will you be back for supper?'

'Maybe. Maybe not.' Caroline's voice was brittle, and Lucy thought that she was near to breaking point behind the calm façade.

When her sister had left she finished the row of beans, drew earth over them and went inside to lay a tray for tea. She shared it alone with her father, and made some more for William when he returned.

'Doesn't Mark want any?' she asked.

William shook his head. 'He went straight off to the hospital, to look at the patients he'll be operating on to-morrow. You know, Lucy, I wouldn't mind being a surgeon myself.'

'I thought you wanted to be an engineer.'

William was gifted at physics and maths and showed every sign of following in his father's footsteps. He screwd his face up, struggling to formulate his thoughts. 'Ye-es. But people might be more interesting than things. Mark says that at my age he wanted to do science. Did you know his father was a Professor of Physics at London University, Lucy?' He was obviously very impressed by this fact.

'No, I didn't. But I'm not really surprised.'

'I expect all his family are brainy,' said William. 'His father wanted him to do physics, but Mark changed his mind in favour of medicine.'

'Plenty of time before you have to decide.' He was still a year from his O-levels and doing splendidly at school. For several terms Lucy had been the one to attend parents' evenings, greatly to William's relief. At fourteen he was very sensitive about the bad impression that his father made on people.

'Mark says the same thing,' he agreed. 'Mark says you should keep your options open as long as possible. He knows about things, doesn't he, Luce?'

Lucy smiled at his earnest young face. William was at an age for hero-worship, and at least Mark was a better influence than the pop stars who guided Susan's life.

William crammed fruit cake into his mouth and spoke again, indistinctly. 'He must be really rich, Luce. You should have seen his new house. It's absolutely super!'

'Bigger than this house?'

'Not bigger, sort of grander. It has a swimming-pool and a tennis court, and stables that he's actually going to use.'

The Grants had stables too, but they had fallen into disrepair many years ago, and were only used for gardening equipment. 'Then I suppose he is rich,' agreed Lucy. 'Or perhaps his fiancée is.' A consultant's salary was quite adequate, she imagined, but Mark was a very new consultant. The sort of house William had described would cost a small fortune today. 'Does Mark have a horse?' she added, and William nodded, frowning slightly, because his hero didn't come up to expectation on this point at least.

'They both do. They go hunting. I told him we're against it.' William had been known to erect barricades across the cart track behind the house, when they heard the hunt in their area.

'And what did he say?'

'He said everyone was entitled to their own opinions.' William's frown deepened and he took another slice of fruit cake. 'He's very nice, Luce, in spite of the hunting. He has an old radio he's going to give me to take to bits. I hope he stays on here until his house is ready. He said he'd like to.'

'I'm not sure his rooms will be free,' Lucy said shortly, because the sooner Mark left the less pain for Caroline. If he didn't go her sister might have to meet the fiancée.

Caroline telephoned at nine o'clock to say that she had

decided to return to the hospital that night. 'All right.' Lucy hesitated, then asked if her sister was on her own.

'Yes.'

'Caro, are you sure you're all right? Are you sure you wouldn't rather come home?'

'And listen to Mark talking about his new house and his fiancée?' Caroline's voice was shrill. She gave a shuddering sob and slammed the telephone down.

Next day Lucy had three lots of people enquiring if she had any rooms free. She would have no trouble filling the two double bedrooms that Mark had taken over, she thought, and decided to ask him when he planned to leave. That evening after supper she knocked on his door. He was sitting in the easy chair by the window, reading the *Journal of British Surgery*.

'Hallo, Lucy. What can I do for you?'

Lucy shut the door behind her. 'Now that the holiday season's getting under way it would help if you could let me know when you're leaving.' At his blank look she added quickly, 'You did say you'd be moving into a hotel when the Barnslow Festival was over.'

He dropped the journal on to the floor and walked over to her side. He topped her by a head, so that she had to look up to him. 'Well, will you be moving next weekend?' she asked, and waited tensely for his answer.

'Have you booked these rooms in advance?'

'No, but——'

'Then I should like to stay, please. If you can put up with me.' His smile was disarming.

'You did say you'd have preferred a hotel.'

'Did I really? When was that?'

'The first day you came. In fact you were pretty blighting altogether.' Lucy felt an urge, which she didn't quite understand, to prick that easy self-assurance.

He looked surprised, then he laughed. 'Was I that bad, little Lucy? I'm afraid I was in a filthy temper, because I'd had a hell of an operating list in the morning, and then that idiot Brown told me the best he could do was a house in the country.'

'Well, thanks,' Lucy said with sarcasm. 'You needn't have made it quite so plain what you thought—both of me and the house.'

He laughed again. 'If you could have seen yourself with your hair pulled back in a ponytail, earth on your face and grubby jeans! You didn't look like the lady of the house!'

'I know I looked awful——' Lucy began crossly.

He tweaked her hair as an elder brother might have done. 'You didn't look awful. You looked sweet, but not very businesslike.'

'I'm immune to flattery.'

He gave an exaggerated sigh. 'If I eat humble pie and beg you to keep me, do you think I might stay?'

'Humble pie isn't your style,' Lucy snapped, annoyed because she had got herself into a tangle. She should have told a white lie, said that the rooms were booked in advance, asked him to vacate them by next Monday.

His expression changed and his eyes narrowed. 'Why are you so upset? What have I said?'

Because she couldn't tell him the truth Lucy said, sorry, she hadn't meant to snap, but that his comments that day had rankled a bit. He apologised again and somehow Lucy found herself saying that of course he could stay if he wanted to. The family would be delighted. All except Caroline and herself, she thought unhappily, as she went downstairs again. Probably Caroline would stay away, at least for the present, until she came to terms with the fact that Mark was not for her.

Now that Mark was staying he unpacked the rest of his belongings, which had previously been stacked in cases and boxes in a corner of his room—books, sports gear, photographs. There was one of a handsome middle-aged couple which took pride of place on the desk, another of a young woman with several small children. His parents? His sister, perhaps?

One day, when he was late leaving for hospital, Lucy arrived with the vacuum cleaner. 'I'm sorry, Mark, I thought you'd gone.'

'My house surgeon telephoned to say the list's been cancelled. Some sort of go-slow.' He sounded annoyed.

'I'll come back later.'

'No need. I'll move into the bedroom.'

She touched the silver-framed photographs. 'Your parents?'

'Yes. My father is dead, and like your father, my mother hasn't really adjusted to the loss. And that's my sister.'

'Not one of your fiancée?' she asked lightly, and he smiled.

'Camilla despises sentiment, but you're right, I ought to have one.'

'Is she medical?' Lucy hoped he wouldn't resent her interest.

'Yes, she is. An anaesthetic registrar. She works at St Anne's hospital in London. We trained together at Q.C.H.'

Then Caroline must know her, at least by sight. 'Will she look for a job in this region now that you've moved, or will she give up when you marry?'

'Good heavens, no!' He looked shocked at the idea. 'Camilla's a very dedicated doctor. She's about to take her F.F.A.'

Lucy knew, from the talk of Caroline and her friends, that the F.F.A. stood for Fellowship of the Faculty of Anaesthetists. So his fiancée must be clever. When she said so he smiled and nodded.

'Yes, Camilla's very bright, and a good examinee.' He sounded extremely proud of her.

'I hope you don't think me terribly nosy,' Lucy murmured.

His mouth quirked. 'Most women are about personal

relations. My mother can't resist a good gossip. If you're interested you'll probably be seeing Camilla tomorrow. She's coming to Barnslow for the day.'

'If you want somewhere really good to eat, the White Heart is the best place for miles around.'

Mark nodded his thanks, and at that moment someone called from the downstairs hall. 'Lucy! Where are you?'

Mrs Rudge's voice! She popped in now and then to see how her protegée was doing and to offer advice. Lucy opened Mark's door and looked over the banister.

'I'm upstairs. I'll be down in a moment,' but Mrs Rudge was already tramping heavily upstairs, puffing a little because she was fat and middle-aged.

Lucy turned back to Mark's door, about to shut it, but Mrs Rudge forestalled her.

'I haven't seen what you've made of your ma's room.' She poked an inquisitive head round the door, stared at Mark and made a breezy apology. 'Sorry, love, thought Lucy was on her own. I like to keep an eye on the girl. Known her since she crawled around in dungarees.'

Once Mrs Rudge started reminiscing it was difficult to stem the flow. Mark, looking irritated, moved towards the bedroom, but Mrs Rudge followed him. 'You don't mind if I peep into the other room? I used to clean it in the old days.'

'I do, actually,' said Mark, at his most forbidding. 'I'm getting ready to go out,' and he shut the door in her face.

Mrs Rudge, looking nonplussed, followed Lucy on to the landing. 'What a rude man! Is he always like that?'

'Only sometimes,' said Lucy, resisting an impulse to laugh and wishing she had the courage to give people the brush-off so firmly. Not that she wanted to get rid of Mrs Rudge, of whom she was very fond, having known her since childhood. Mrs Rudge might be a terrible talker, but she was very kind. She genuinely wanted to help.

Lucy took her into the kitchen and made coffee. Drinking it, Mrs Rudge brooded on Lucy's lodger. 'A surgeon, is he?' She looked impressed. 'They're always like that, aren't they? Masterful! He reminds me of that good-looking actor in that hospital series ...' She rambled on, then returned to Lucy's affairs. 'Seeing how you've no man to advise you, dear, I'd be a bit careful with your gentleman guests.'

Lucy stared, and Mrs Rudge leant forward to make her point more forcefully. 'I shouldn't go into their rooms except when they're out, not the young ones anyway. You're a very pretty girl and men can get the wrong idea.'

'Mrs Rudge!' exclaimed Lucy, outraged and angry. She calmed down and added, 'You're being quite absurd. The man's engaged. We were talking about his fiancée.'

'Who isn't here, is she?' Mrs Rudge countered, not a scrap offended by Lucy's manner. 'No need to bite my head off, love. If you think about it you'll realise I'm right.'

Lucy looked forward with considerable interest to meeting Camilla, though it was possible she might not want to come out to the house. Mark left early for work in an exceptionally good mood, and by nine in the evening it looked as if they were not coming. The family were grouped around the television, watching the news, when there was a knock on the kitchen door and Mark stood there, a young woman behind him.

A tall slim young woman, who held herself superbly. She looked a year or two younger than Mark, which would put her in the late twenties, and was elegant rather than pretty, with a high-bridged nose and an unmistakable aura of breeding and wealth. Just the sort of person she would have expected Mark to choose, thought Lucy. Someone as assured and successful as he was. A match for him intellectually, and good-looking too, if you liked her style. Camilla had blonde hair cut very short, to show off a shapely head, and an excellent complexion.

'I hope we're not interrupting,' said Mark.

'Of course not.' Lucy switched the television off and there were introductions all round.

Camilla was smiling, gracious and very slightly patronising. She didn't sit down, so neither did Mark, and after a few minutes of conversation they left.

Susan started to rave. 'Some day I'm going to look like that! Smooth! And really cool! Did you see that dress? And those shoes? They must have cost a bomb.'

'She's not as pretty as Lucy,' William said loyally, and Lucy smiled at him, touched by this remark. She knew she was nice-looking, without being dazzlingly pretty like young Susan. Shining brown hair and clear hazel eyes made quite a pleasing combination, and her complexion was as good as Camilla's. Now why was she making a comparison?

Susan reacted to William's remark with scorn. 'Of course Lucy's prettier, but Camilla's got something more important. She has style.' She peered into the kitchen mirror and twisted a red-gold curl around one finger. 'I wish I had a figure like hers,' she added enviously.

Susan was sixteen and still had her puppy fat. 'Don't worry, darling, you'll slim down in a year or two,' Lucy assured her. She switched on the television again and sat down to watch the end of the news. At eleven-thirty, when she had gone to bed, Lucy heard Mark's car drive off and return a long time later. She wondered where Camilla was staying.

'She has friends in Shrewsbury,' Mark said next morning. 'She knows this area quite well.'

That afternoon, when Lucy was fetching in the washing, a smart little sports car drew into the courtyard and Camilla stepped out. She wore grey slacks and a beautifully cut blue suede jacket, that exactly matched her eyes. Lucy walked to meet her, a pile of clothes in her arms.

'I'm afraid Mark's out.'

'I know that, Miss Grant. He asked me to collect something.'

'Do you mind coming in the back way? The front door's locked.' They passed through the kitchen. In the hall Camilla halted, one well manicured hand on the stair rail.

'I know the way, thank you, Miss Grant, I'm sure you have a lot to do.' Her blue eyes rested on the pile of clothes in the other girl's arms.

The princess and the peasant, thought Lucy, with a spurt of resentment. She nodded and turned away, wondering what it was about Camilla Fielding that irritated her so much. To be honest perhaps it was just plain old-fashioned envy. The girl had wealth and sophistication, quite apart from her status as a professional woman. Lucy wondered what sort of family she came from, how long Mark had been in love with her. He must have known her for years if they had trained at the same hospital, even if she had been his junior. Lucy thought what a pity it was that Camilla hadn't stayed at Q.C.H. If she had done so, probably everyone would have known about her and Mark, and Caroline would have realised sooner that she was wasting her time trying to attract him.

She decided to offer the other girl some tea, so she kept the kitchen door open and when Camilla came downstairs a few minutes later, she went to meet her. 'Would you care for tea, Dr Fielding? I'm just about to have some.'

Camilla glanced at her watch, while Lucy studied her sapphire engagement ring .'Thanks, Miss Grant, I should like some.'

Lucy sat her down in the dining-room and returned soon after with a tea-tray.

'This cake is delicious,' Camilla said graciously. 'Mark says you're an excellent cook. He seems very comfortable here, though I'm surprised he hasn't moved into a hotel.'

'So am I. He intended to originally.'

Camilla shrugged. 'You know what men are like. They

can't be bothered once they're settled. He could have had a room at the White Hart now the Festival's over, but he says he prefers it here.' I can't think why, her look implied, as her gaze wandered round the pleasant but homely room. Marsh House was a delightful old place, but the White Hart was a four-star hotel.

Lucy hoped she wasn't going to see much of Camilla. 'How's your new house going?' she asked. 'Mark's told me about it.'

Again those raised eyebrows. 'Good heavens,' thought Lucy in amazement, 'she doesn't think a peasant like me should call him by his Christian name.'

'Slowly, I'm afraid,' said Camilla. She finished her tea and rose. 'Thank you, Miss Grant, I mustn't keep you from your work.'

Next day, when Lucy dusted Mark's rooms, there was a photograph of Camilla on his bedside table. She was wearing formal riding clothes and she looked magnificent, standing slim and proud beside her horse.

'Yes, she's a splendid rider,' said Mark, when Lucy asked him about the picture. 'She competes in show jumping events when she has the time. Used to do more before she qualified.'

He sounded very proud of her, as well he might do, for he was marrying a very talented young woman. Lucy wished that she could like her better, though it didn't really matter. Once Mark left they were not likely to meet. The Franklins and the Grants would move in different social circles.

Caroline stayed away for a week, then telephoned to say she was bringing a friend back to supper. The friend was a doctor from the hospital, Henry Wilson. 'He works in anaesthetics,' Caroline told them.

Lucy took to Henry. He was cheerful, friendly and obviously fond of Caroline. He could be the fillip she needed to restore her shattered morale. Outwardly her sister was back to normal, but Caroline took care that she was not alone with Lucy.

It was Henry who brought up the subject of Mark Franklin. 'Caroline says he's staying here. Don't you find him rather ... daunting? I'm not sure that's the right word, but you must know what I mean.'

Lucy glanced at her sister, but Caroline's face gave nothing away. 'He can be a bit overpowering,' she agreed, 'But he's nice when you get to know him.'

Henry nodded. 'He's a great chap. I anaesthetise for him twice a week. Now that I'm no longer frightened of him I enjoy the challenge, but he was quite a shock after the dear old boy he replaced.' His smile was a little rueful, as if recalling tense moments in the operating theatre. 'You knew him at Queen's, didn't you?' he added to Caroline.

'That's right,' Caroline said neutrally.

'His fiancée came the other night,' Susan volunteered. 'My word!' and she rolled her eyes expressively.

'What was she like?' Henry asked with interest. 'Very pretty?'

Susan hesitated, searching for the right words, so Lucy supplied them. 'Not pretty, no. Good-looking. Very classy. Very county.'

'It fits,' murmured Henry. 'Franklin's quite obviously from the same sort of background. And money marries money, doesn't it?'

Caroline rose abruptly and went to the sink. She made a business of sorting out the dirty dishes and Henry joined her.

'You wash and I'll dry,' he said, tying Caroline's apron round her slender waist and dropping a kiss on her cheek.

He was really a very nice young man, thought Lucy. If only her sister would show more interest in him, but a flicker of irritation had crossed her face at his kiss. Lucy hoped that Caroline wasn't just using him to prove that she didn't care about Mark. While the others were watching television she managed a few quiet words.

'He's nice, Caro. I'm glad you brought him.'

'He's all right,' Caroline shrugged, 'but he's too easy-going. He'll never make the grade as a consultant if he doesn't push a bit harder.'

'And that's so important?'

'Of course it is! Of course!' Caroline admired success. she had no time for amiable nonentities. She leant closer to Lucy. 'Is Mark in?'

'No, he's out for the evening.'

Caroline nodded and left the room. A few minutes later she came back, looking strained and unhappy. When Henry and she were preparing to leave she hung back for a last word with Lucy. 'I saw her photo, and I know her by sight. Lord Fielding's daughter.' There was bitterness in her voice.

'Lord ... Her father's a lord?' That explained the haughty air perhaps.

'A medical lord,' Caroline explained wearily. 'He was Sir Richard Fielding until last year's Honours List.'

'Is he at Q.C.H?'

'No, at the postgraduate place. I heard him lecture once and he's absolutely brilliant.' Caroline rubbed her forehead, her face strained and unhappy. 'It won't be exactly a disadvantage to have Lord Fielding as your father-in-law!' She sounded defeated and hopeless, and Lucy's heart ached for her sister.

'Oh, Caro, I'm so sorry, but it's better that you accept things. Mark's not for you. He never could have been.'

'Has he told you when they're getting married?'

'No,' Lucy said slowly. 'I don't think they've fixed a date yet. He said Camilla wants to take her F.F.A. before she leaves St Anne's hospital.'

Caroline's face brightened. 'So it could be some time. Perhaps they'll drift apart.' There was renewed hope in her voice and she gave Lucy a bright-eyed feverish glance. 'What a fool she is, not making sure of him while she can. Coming, Henry!' and she darted away from her sister.

So she was not going to be sensible. Her last words didn't imply that she had given up. Girls in love could make such fools of themselves, even clever girls like Caroline.

CHAPTER FOUR

'THAT'S a nice piano in your sitting-room,' Mark said one evening. 'Any objection if I play it?'

He had come to join Lucy in the vegetable garden, where she was transplanting young cabbages. She smiled up at him, happy because she was doing the work she most enjoyed, outdoor work rather than jobs in the house.

'Of course you can. Pianos are best used. It was bought for my mother. She played very well.' And Lucy had inherited it, though she didn't mention this. She seldom talked about music these days. She sometimes played when there was no one else around, though now that the sitting-room was given over to the visitors, that was a rare event.

'Don't get the idea that I'm any good,' Mark said with a smile, 'but I find it relaxing.'

'Then the more you play the better,' Lucy observed. 'You must have just about the most unrelaxing job in the world!' She knew from what Caroline had told her that when things went wrong in the operating theatre, the surgeon in charge was under tremendous stress. If Mark was sometimes brusque and bad-tempered perhaps he had more excuse than most men.

As always he read her thoughts accurately. 'Am I that bad?' he asked wryly. 'You're not much good at relaxing yourself, my dear Lucy. Don't you ever stop working?'

'It's such a beautiful evening, and I enjoy gardening.'

'I can see that.' He smiled as he leant forward to remove a leaf from her hair. 'You're a very pretty girl, Lucy Grant, and this is your natural setting.' He gestured around him at the lush and fertile garden.

Lucy's heart gave an odd little thump. 'You mean I

look the part with a trug in my hand?' She made a joke
of it because Mark's words had taken her by surprise.
His closeness was having an odd effect on her breathing.
'Bucolic and buxom? Is that what you mean?'

She stood up. Mark's eyes went over her slim figure, clad
in the inevitable shirt and jeans. 'I meant nothing of the
sort,' he said shortly. 'You should learn to accept a compli-
ment more gracefully. You shouldn't be so diffident.'

'Diffident!' No one had called her that before.

Lucy went down on her knees again and dropped a young
cabbage plant into the hole she had prepared, wishing he
would go away. When he didn't she repeated the word
again. 'Diffident! Is that how you really think of me? It's
certainly not a word anyone would apply to *you*!'

She was getting quite worked up about it and Mark
laughed. 'Sorry, my dear girl, I didn't mean to offend
you. You're a bit edgy tonight. Any reason?'

She could hardly tell him that it was due to his presence,
so she said nothing. Mark stared down at her, then spoke
again. 'Perhaps you're tired. Or in need of some fun. When
did you last have an evening out?'

'Not for some time,' Lucy admitted. 'But I'm going to
the residents' party on Friday.'

The junior medical staff at Barnslow General were giving a farewell party for two of their colleagues. Caroline
had suggested that she come, and Lucy, who knew a good
many of the young doctors, was looking forward to it.

'Good,' said Mark. 'I've been invited myself, though
I'm not sure if I'll go.'

'Not grand enough for you, Mr Franklin?'

His hand closed on her shoulder and he gave her a little
shake. 'You want to watch that sharp tongue of yours, my
girl! I happen to be on duty on Friday night,' and he turned
and walked off with his light springy step.

Lucy watched him disappear through the gap in the
stone wall, her expression thoughtful. She had grown used
to having him around. There was no doubt that he lent

colour to a rather dull existence, for he had the sort of personality that you couldn't overlook. She would miss him when he left, and that was a surprising admission in view of her initial dislike of him. In fact there was no immediate prospect of him leaving, for the builders were proceeding at a snail's pace, according to Mark.

'The usual story—taking on too much work and trying to keep all their customers happy. I know they're not at my place every day, but what can I do about it? I'm too busy to keep chasing them up.'

He had sounded very frustrated when he told them this, and Lucy had thought what a pity it was that Camilla hadn't given up her job in London. Surely she could work for her exams in Barnslow? Surely their new house and Mark's happiness should take priority over her career? Part of Mark's moodiness these days must be because he was missing his fiancée. Since they both had demanding jobs they could meet only occasionally. Lucy remembered Caroline's words about the pair drifting apart, and began to wonder if it might be more than just wishful thinking.

Henry Wilson arrived to pick Lucy up on Friday instead of Caroline. 'She had a last-minute admission,' he explained. 'You're looking great, Lucy! I like that dress.'

Lucy had taken pains with her appearance, and even if the dress was last year's, she knew it suited her. It was soft and feminine, in a pretty shade of blue, with little ruffles at neck and wrists. Not for her the tailored clothes Caroline preferred.

There were quite a few other men who said much the same as Henry that evening. Lucy loved dancing and went out so seldom that she enjoyed herself doubly when she did. The stereo system in the big residents' lounge thumped out the latest dance and Lucy gyrated with enthusiasm, a broad smile on her face. The music came to an end and she collapsed on to a sofa with her partner, laughing and breathless.

'That was quite a performance,' a deep voice said from behind her, and she turned quickly to look up at Mark. He had just come in, accompanied by one of the consultant anaesthetists. A house surgeon was handing him a drink, telling him how pleased they were he'd made it. Several young doctors gathered around him and Lucy noticed with faint surprise that he seemed very popular.

When he moved away she commented on this to her partner, a house physician on the same unit as Caroline. The young man nodded. 'Great chap, Franklin. I'm hoping to do his job when I finish my present stint.'

'I should have thought he could be a bit . . . overpowering at times. Not an easy man to work for?'

'Too true,' agreed the house physician. 'But that's what makes his job so stimulating. It's a challenge, don't you see. And he's a hundred per cent straight. If you muck things up he'll tear a strip off you, not run you down behind your back, like my present revered chief.'

'I can just imagine him tearing strips off people,' Lucy agreed with a smile, eyeing Mark's tall figure across the crowded room. 'You must be a real glutton for punishment.'

'But he can be awfully nice too,' said the young man ingenuously. 'My friend, who works for him at the moment, says he's marvellous with old people. And the kids adore him. So that proves my point, doesn't it? He must be a decent type.'

Lucy thought of William, who didn't give his allegiance lightly, and had to agree with the young doctor. The evening wore on. She watched Caroline attach herself to the group around Mark, wondered if he would ask her sister to dance, noticed that he didn't, and saw him leave about ten.

'Bored by a residents' party,' she suggested to the house physician, who had sought her out again.

The young man shook his head. 'Franklin's not like that. He has a case to do in Theatre,' which made Lucy feel that she had been ungenerous in her judgment.

At midnight she felt that she had had enough, but couldn't find Caroline or Henry. Not for the first time she regretted that they had been forced to sell the family car, for she hated having to ask for lifts from people, and there would be no buses at this hour. Half the residents seemed to have gone off on their night rounds, and the ones who were left were people she didn't know particularly well.

For something to do she went over to the piano that stood in one corner of the room. It was battered and scratched, but to her surprise it was in tune. She played one or two pieces softly for her own amusement, Chopin, Schumann, and then someone came over and asked her if she knew the theme tune of a recent film hit. Lucy had a good ear and a retentive memory, and there was applause when she ended. People gathered round and their requests came one after another. It changed to a lively singsong, then a Welshman with an excellent tenor voice gave a spirited rendering of a Verdi aria. As the last notes died away he seized Lucy by the hand, drew her to her feet, and planted an enthusiastic kiss on her cheek.

'Lovely playing, that was! We must do it again some time.'

'Lovely singing too.' Lucy smiled back at him, flushed and happy. 'Has anyone seen my sister? It's time I went home.'

'I'll take you home.' Mark rose from the armchair where he had been sitting. Lucy hadn't seen him come in, so engrossed had she been in music-making.

'Shall we go?' he asked, slipping a hand through her arm.

As they went out she heard a woman's comment, brittle-voiced and spiteful, 'I wonder what his fiancée would say!' and a man's reply.

'He's only taking her home, Jane.'

Mark heard it too. His lips compressed. 'The bad side of hospital life—gossip and intrigue! If that young woman ever applies for a job on my firm she won't get it.'

He sounded more annoyed than such a trivial remark warranted. When Lucy said as much he frowned and shook his head. 'I detest that sort of mischief-making. Medical marriages are more vulnerable than most—the hours we work, our close association with nurses. And in the case of Camilla and me the fact that we may be working in different hospitals for a long time yet, that we only see each other when we're off duty.'

Lucy stared at him. 'But surely ... Camilla will be working at Barnslow once you're married?'

'There won't be any consultant anaesthetist posts coming up here for several years,' he said shortly. He unlocked the car door and waited for her to get in.

'Must it be a consultant's job?' Lucy asked, and he shrugged irritably.

'Once she has her F.F.A. she won't want to continue as a registrar. There's a job coming up at Westhampton, but that's not until next March.'

'But Westhampton's miles away!'

'I know.' As the car moved on to the main road he said slowly. 'A girl like Camilla is perfectly capable of combining marriage and a career. It would be a ridiculous waste of her training if she gave up.' He sounded as if he was talking more to convince himself than to inform Lucy. He looked tense and unhappy, and she longed to comfort him.

'Then if the job at Westhampton's not until March you could have a few months together when you first get married. When *are* you getting married, Mark?'

'Autumn if the house is ready in time. But I can't see Camilla sitting at home for six months,' he observed, smiling faintly at the thought.

Frustrated he might be at the present set-up, but he was the sort of modern-minded man who wouldn't want a homely little wife. Their marriage would be an efficient partnership of two highly intelligent, very able people. For some reason the idea depressed Lucy. She wondered if Camilla would be gentle with Mark, when he came home tired from a gruelling day in the operating theatre, or depressed because he had been unable to save a patient's life. Or would she have so many problems of her own that Mark would have to do the comforting?

As they drove along Mark removed one hand from the steering wheen and tapped her on the knee. 'You're full of surprises, Lucy. Where did you learn to play the piano like that? You put my efforts to shame.'

'I've had some musical training,' she said briefly.

'In Barnslow?'

'No, in London.'

When he probed she answered reluctantly, and Mark made an exasperated sound. 'What a funny girl you are! Why do you dislike talking about yourself so much?'

She bit her lip. 'Only about this, because it's so important. Please drop it, Mark.'

'If that's what you want,' he said brusquely, and after that they were silent for the rest of the short drive home.

Mark parked in the barn, and while he was locking the car, Lucy heard the telephone ringing. It was nearly one o'clock and the rest of the family would be in bed. She dashed indoors and snatched up the receiver, hoping it hadn't woken them. Camilla! Lucy recognised that clear incisive voice at once.

'If you'll hang on, Miss Fielding, Mark won't be a moment. We've only just got back——'

'We?' Camilla cut in sharply, and Lucy cursed her unthinking remark.

'There was a party at the hospital, and Mark gave me a lift home.' She heard approaching footsteps. 'Here he is,' and when Mark appeared she handed him the receiver.

As she left the room she heard his opening words. 'Did you have to ring so late, darling? You rang earlier? I'm sorry, but I did tell you about tonight.'

Lucy closed the door quietly and went upstairs to bed.

Mark had sounded irritated, so Camilla was being difficult. There had been an edge to her voice when she spoke to Lucy. She hadn't liked the idea of her fiancée driving home another girl. The fact that she could be jealous made her seem more human, and in an odd sort of way, more likeable.

Lucy stared at her reflection in the bedroom mirror as she removed her make-up. Her morale had been boosted by her success this evening, but she was no threat to Camilla, she knew that very well. Mark had remarked that she was pretty, that evening in the vegetable garden. He had spoken lightly, smilingly, as he might have done to a young sister. He seemed to like her, but he loved Camilla. What would it be like to have a man like Mark in love with you? Lucy drew her bedroom curtains and threw open the bottom of the window. What would it be like to have Mark in love with you?

'I've had too much to drink, Beryl!' Lucy bent to pat the old dog, who always slept on the floor by the side of her bed. She switched off the light, pulled the bedclothes around her, and lay listening for Mark to come upstairs.

It was a long time before he did so. Had he been on the telephone until now? Had Camilla been hard to placate? Much more likely they had been discussing whatever had caused the girl to ring in the first place. As she settled down to sleep, Lucy's last clear thought was that she spent too much time thinking about Mark's affairs. It was a bad habit which she must do her best to break.

On Saturdays Lucy allowed the family to sleep in, though she was up at the usual time herself. There were two other visitors beside Mark, and they had asked for an early breakfast. She was clearing away their dishes when Mark appeared.

'Sorry I'm late. Don't bother to cook me anything. I'll just have cereal.'

When she carried the tray out he followed her into the

kitchen. 'Have you had breakfast? No? Then I'll eat in here with you.'

'You don't have to.'

'But I want to,' he said firmly, seating himself at the big table.

He was on duty this weekend, she knew. 'Will Camilla be coming down?' she asked.

Mark's face darkened and his mouth compressed. 'No,' he said shortly, and picked up the local paper.

While she prepared breakfast he thumbed through the local advertisements. 'Looking for anything in particular?' she asked.

'A garden centre. Is there one near here?'

'Yes, I'll give you directions and you could go there next time Camilla comes down.'

'I'll go on my own.' He sounded thoroughly fed up, and Lucy felt very sorry for him. He was in love and wanted to get married. This period, of getting their house and garden ready, should have been shared by Mark and Camilla. The girl must be blind if she couldn't see that.

'Mark.' She turned the bacon over while she spoke. 'Please don't think I'm interfering, but your present life is so obviously unsatisfactory.' He stiffened and she went on quickly, 'You *do* think I'm interfering, so I'd better shut up.'

He gave her one of his very direct looks, then he smiled and shook his head. 'It's all right, Lucy. You're easy to talk to and I need to let off steam. What's on your mind exactly?'

'Couldn't you persuade Camilla to give up her present job? Move down here? Get married sooner? Surely there are locums going in the summer months, with so many doctors on holiday?'

He was silent, thinking about it. 'There might be,' he agreed, 'but where would we live? The house is chaotic.'

'You could get a couple of rooms ready, camp out. It would be fun.'

'I don't think living surrounded by builders would be Camilla's idea of fun.'

'But surely if it was only for a limited time ... well, all right then, a hospital apartment or a hotel ... or—or even here?' She looked at him doubtfully, thinking she must have been mad to suggest such an idea. Camilla would scorn the idea of staying in the Grants' house. When he was silent she tried again. 'There must be some way, Mark. If I was her——' She broke off at his sudden frown and went very red. 'If I was Camilla,' she had been going to say, 'If I was in love I'd be prepared to put up with a bit of discomfort. I wouldn't care where I lived.' For surely being together mattered more than anything else, even to a career woman like Camilla?

She slid the bacon and eggs on to a plate and carried it over to Mark, poured coffee and sat down opposite him.

'I told you I didn't want anything,' he said ungraciously.

'Well, I've made it, so you might as well eat it. Mark, is there something wrong, more than just life in general? Did I speak out of turn just now?'

He sighed. 'My dear girl, you were trying to be helpful, and I appreciate your interest. If you spoke out of turn it was last night, not this morning.' His expression was wry and Lucy suddenly remembered.

'Oh dear! I'd forgotten! I'm afraid I dropped a brick when I answered the telephone. I shouldn't have said you brought me back from the party, should I?'

'It would have been better if you hadn't,' he agreed moodily.

'Oh, Mark, I'm so sorry. I didn't mean to make trouble.' He didn't answer and she leant forward anxiously. 'I just didn't think—you must believe me.'

He took his time about replying, then suddenly exploded, making Lucy jump in her chair and slop her coffee. 'Women!' he exclaimed, banging the table hard with the flat of his hand. 'I thought Camilla had more sense. Anyone would think I'd taken you to the damn party, instead of merely brought you home, because we live in the same house.'

He looked angry and upset, and Lucy felt very guilty, especially as he had no chance of making it up with Camilla, if he was on duty for the weekend.

'Perhaps,' she said slowly, 'it's not just the party. Perhaps she doesn't like you living here at all.' The idea had only just occurred to her. Would she like it, if she was engaged to Mark, and he was staying in a house run by an unattached young woman?

Mark gave a contemptuous snort. 'Then she's a complete fool. I can't stand possessive women!'

That didn't sound very loverlike. Lucy looked anxiously at him. 'I'm sorry if you had a row last night, especially as it was all my fault.'

He passed his coffee cup for a refill. 'You may have triggered it off,' he said grimly, 'but we've been heading for one ever since I came to Barnslow. I can't understand— I simply cannot understand—how a woman of Camilla's intelligence can be so idiotic.'

'I don't think intelligence counts when your emotions are involved,' said Lucy. 'Mark, when you see her next, try and persuade her to move down here.'

'She wouldn't agree. She expects to start her married life in the sort of place she grew up in.'

'And what was that like?'

His expression was sardonic. 'The Manor's a show place in Berkshire. It's been in the Fielding family for generations. And they have a superb apartment in London as well, in one of those roads off Hyde Park.'

An apartment in the West End and a country house in Berkshire! Lucy began to understand why Camilla might be hard to please. 'I do see the problems, but if she loves you I'm sure she'll try to adapt.'

'Camilla has no intention of adapting,' he snapped, then sighed and pushed his chair back. 'I shouldn't be talking to you like this, but I know you'll keep it to yourself.' He looked more vulnerable than he usually did. He had run a hand through his hair, so that it fell forward into his eyes. He looked boyish, unhappy and extremely attractive, so that Lucy felt a strong urge to comfort him.

'Don't spend all weekend being angry with each other. Make it up as soon as possible. Ring her before you go out.' She leant towards him and he smiled as he studied her earnest young face.

'What a nice girl you are, Lucy. I think I'll try your advice.'

Later, as he was leaving for the hospital, he passed her in the hall. 'I telephoned, but she's gone out for the day. Pity!' He nodded at the flower arrangement on the hall table. 'You have a talent for that. Goodbye, my dear.'

Lucy fitted the last of the lupins into place and stood back to survey them. Mark had looked strained and unhappy. He had almost certainly slept badly, and a man with the sort of responsibility he carried, needed to relax when he was off duty. If only he had picked a nice ordinary girl, or if he had to pick a medical woman, someone who would put his career before her own. Such women did exist. Her mother had been friendly with a married woman anaesthetist at Barnslow General, who organised a part-time career very successfully around a richly satisfying family life.

What had attracted Mark to Camilla? Had her background been a factor, as Caroline had hinted? Was Mark the sort of man who would marry for money and position? Did he even need to do so? Caroline had said that he was brilliant, with an assured future, and he came from an academic family himself. For that matter why had he been content to settle for a provincial hospital, when he might have waited for a vacancy in a teaching hospital?

Frowning over these thoughts, Lucy went upstairs to make the beds, quite forgetting what she had decided only

last night—that Mark's affairs were none of her business.
That it was foolish to get so involved with one of her
visitors.

He came back for lunch and sat in the garden all afternoon, within earshot of the telephone. He was eating tea
with the family when he had a call from his registrar.

'Sounds like a bleeding ulcer,' he told Caroline, who
was home for the weekend, and to Lucy, 'Don't wait supper
for me.'

Saturday night supper was a scratch meal, eaten around
the television. Lucy was doing the dishes when the front
door bell rang.

'Would you answer it, William?'

He was back soon, looking disgusted. 'It's that woman—
Mark's fiancée. I didn't know she was coming.'

'Neither did I.' Lucy dried her hands and went through
to the hall, while Caroline rose as if to follow her, then
sat down again.

Camilla stood there, wearing the suede jacket that Lucy
admired and very much on her dignity. 'Good evening,
Miss Grant. Your brother says my fiancé is out.'

'Yes, Miss Fielding, but I think he'll be back soon. He
had an urgent call from the hospital.'

Camilla gave a thin smile. 'Then I'll wait in his room.'
Her manner was haughty in the extreme, but Lucy sensed
her inner tension. If she had come down without warning
she might not be too sure of her welcome.

'Have you had any supper, Miss Fielding?' she asked.
'Would you care for a hot drink?'

Camilla admitted that it was some time since she had
eaten, so Lucy offered to bring her something on a tray.
She found it difficult to like the other girl, but this was
Mark's fiancée, so she felt she should make the effort. She
sliced cold chicken, took salad ingredients from the crisper
and added a couple of bread rolls. A glass of cold milk?
She poured it and took the tray upstairs.

Caroline was prowling round Mark's room, clearly on

edge. Lucy put the tray down on the low table in the window.

'I'm sure he'll be back soon. Do have something to eat while you're waiting.'

Camilla stared at the food. 'Thank you,' she said absently, her mind presumably on her coming meeting with Mark.

It was obvious that she was in no mood for conversation, so Lucy left her to it and went downstairs to face a barrage of questions and comments from the family.

'What does she want?' asked William.

'What a stupid time to come!' exclaimed Caroline.

'What's she wearing?' from Susan.

'One at a time,' Lucy murmured. 'How do I know what she wants? To see Mark, obviously. They are engaged, after all.'

'I'm sure he didn't know she was coming,' said Caroline, 'or he'd have mentioned it to us. I shouldn't think he'll be particularly pleased to see her. He'll be tired after operating so late.'

'You hope,' muttered William, and Caroline rounded angrily on him.

'Go to bed, you little beast!'

Lucy followed her young brother into the hall. 'Did that crack mean anything special?' she asked under her breath.

William's blue eyes were wide and innocent. 'You know how Caro feels about him.'

'Has Susan been gossiping?'

'Sue? No, I worked it out for myself. She's hoping they'll break up, isn't she? P'raps they will too.' He grinned cheekily and started up the stairs, leaving Lucy worried and unhappy.

If Susan and William had guessed that Caroline was in love with Mark, how many other people might have reached the same conclusion? Her colleagues? The nurses? Even Mark himself? Her sister was laying herself wide open to humiliation, if she persisted in her present course.

Lucy opened the front door and took a deep breath of the evening air. It was June now, nearly the longest day, and she wandered round the garden in the half light, reluctant to go indoors again. When Mark's car turned into the courtyard she was leaning on the wall by the pear tree. She stayed there unseen, as he drove into the barn, locked up and came out again. She had half an idea of telling him about Camilla's arrival, so that he would be prepared in advance, when the front door was flung open and Camilla ran out.

'Mark?' She halted for a moment, peering about her, then she hurried towards him and Lucy stepped back quickly into the shelter of some bushes. She heard Mark's astonished exclamation, Camilla's little half sob, half laugh, then silence. As she made her way round the side of the house, she paused for a moment by the back door and looked back. She could just see them in the dim light, locked in each other's arms, kissing passionately.

She felt ashamed that she had looked, had intruded even that far on their privacy. Biting her lip, she went into the kitchen, to find Caroline and Susan still there.

'Are the lovers reunited?' asked Caroline with brittle sarcasm.

Lucy nodded. 'They're in the garden. I wonder if he wants anything to eat.'

'Shall I go and ask?' Susan jumped up with unusual alacrity. She adored Mark and admired Camilla, following the progress of their love affair with almost as much interest as she devoted to the affairs of the pop stars.

'No! Leave them alone, Sue. He can ask, can't he?'

Lucy dropped into a chair and stared at the figures on the television screen, her thoughts with the couple in the garden. Some time later Mark came to the kitchen alone. He looked very tired, but happier than he had done in the morning. He said he had eaten at the hospital.

'But thanks for feeding Camilla.' A moment's hesitation, then he asked if one of the single rooms was free. Lucy nodded. 'Then may she have it? She forgot to make any arrangements.' He smiled as he said it, as if it was unusual for Camilla to be so unpractical.

Caroline shifted in her chair. Lucy hesitated, caught her eye, but could think of no reason for refusing. 'I'll make the bed up,' she said, and followed him upstairs.

When she showed Camilla the room, the girl glanced around it with what Lucy had labelled her haughty look. It was small and more simply furnished than Mark's room, but the other visitors had seemed quite satisfied with it.

'I suppose it'll do,' Camilla said carelessly, 'though I'd have preferred my own bathroom.'

'You can use Mark's,' Lucy suggested, restraining herself from snapping. 'After all, it is only for one night.'

'I might be staying longer,' Camilla answered. 'Mark wants me to see the builders on Monday, get them to concentrate on a few rooms. Then we can set a date for the wedding.' Her tone was complacent and she stared at Lucy as she spoke.

'I'm afraid you won't be able to stay here after Sunday,' Lucy said quietly. 'The room is booked.'

Camilla ran a comb through her hair, smiling into the mirror as she spoke. 'That's all right, Miss Grant. Then I'll have to use the sofa in his sitting-room, won't I?' The smile grew. 'Though the bed would be more comfortable.' She turned the sapphire engagement ring on her finger. 'You wouldn't think Mark would be so stuffy, would you? He insisted I sleep here tonight.'

Lucy walked towards the door, her colour heightened, for something about the other girl's manner was subtly offensive. 'I expect he thought it would set a bad example to that young sister of yours,' Camilla added, and Lucy shut the door on her quickly, glad to get away.

It was nothing to her what Mark and Camilla did! Most engaged people made love; it was an accepted fact these days, though her father's generation might not approve. Then why had the girl been so anxious to underline the point? Surely someone as pleased with herself as Camilla appeared to be, so self-confident and successful, so soon to be married, could not still be dwelling on last night's incident?

'She's just making sure,' Lucy thought wryly, as she climbed the stairs to her own room, 'making sure I've got the message that Mark is most definitely hers.'

Next morning Caroline got up earlier than she usually did on her weekends off duty. She joined Lucy in the kitchen, looking as if she hadn't had much sleep.

'Why didn't you sleep in?' Lucy asked her.

Caroline's eyes were on the half open door to the dining-room. 'I've been awake since six.'

There were footsteps in the hall, and Mark and Camilla walked into the dining-room, casually dressed both of them, tall, good-looking, a well matched pair.

Caroline stared avidly, her face taut. 'She's just as I remembered from seeing her around Q.C.H. Anyone would look good in those clothes, wouldn't they? Introduce me, Lucy. I might as well get it over.'

The two girls went into the dining-room. Caroline had herself well under control now, said the right things and left when Lucy did.

'Much as I expected,' she commented, standing beside Lucy while her sister fried bacon. 'Rich, spoilt and superior! What can Mark see in her?'

Lucy sighed, for she was beginning to find Caroline tiresome. 'He sees her differently, of course. He's in love with her. She doesn't treat *him* like a peasant!' She tried to make a joke of it, but Caroline didn't smile.

'It won't last,' she said confidently. 'She'll always put her career first, you'll see.'

'You can't possibly know that. And they're going to fix a wedding date soon. She told me last night.'

Mark left Camilla sitting on the lawn with the Sunday papers, while he went to the hospital to check on last night's admissions. At eleven Camilla wandered inside, glanced into the downstairs sitting-room and retreated when she saw that it was occupied. They were the only other visitors, a pleasant middle-aged couple who were staying for the weekend.

Lucy was topping up the water, in the vase on the old oak chest in the hall. Her grip on the water jug tightened, because she never felt at ease with Camilla. 'Would you care for some coffee? I've just given the others some.'

'Thank you. I should like it outside, please.' Not for Camilla Mark's friendly habit of joining the family in the kitchen!

Lucy carried out a small tray and set it down on the bench where Camilla was sitting. Caroline and Susan had gone off to play tennis, and her father was still in bed. The garden was bright with sunshine, peaceful, beautiful, but Camilla looked less pleased with herself than she had done last night.

'I can't think why Mark's not back yet,' she said irritably.

'Something unexpected must have cropped up. Medicine's not like other jobs, is it?' Lucy spoke from experience of Caroline and her colleagues.

'I know that, Miss Grant!' snapped Camilla. 'I am a doctor, after all.' She frowned over her coffee and added, more to herself than to Lucy, 'He has a rotten registrar, who's not prepared to accept any responsibility—calls Mark in for every emergency.'

Lucy had met the young man in question, who was a friend of Henry Wilson's. She had liked him, and felt that Camilla's judgment was unkind. 'He's new to the job, isn't he? He hasn't had much experience yet.'

Camilla shrugged that off contemptuously. 'He shouldn't be in surgery if he's frightened of responsibility. I wouldn't tolerate that sort of attitude from my juniors.'

She was a senior registrar, Lucy knew, which was only one grade below a consultant. It was hard to imagine

Camilla being anything but heartily disliked by her younger colleagues. 'Will you be working at Barnslow after you're married?' she asked.

Camilla shrugged again, and said, as Mark had already done, 'None of the anaesthetists are due to retire for several years, but a job will be coming up at Westhampton in the New Year.'

'Isn't that too far away?'

'I should have to sleep in for my nights on call,' Camilla admitted.

'And you wouldn't mind that?' To Lucy it seemed an odd arrangement for a newly married woman. 'Mark wouldn't prefer you to work nearer home?'

'Of course he'd prefer it,' Camilla said impatiently, as if Lucy was being very obtuse, 'but there isn't a job going, so he'll have to put up with it.'

'General practice?'

'Not on your life!' Camilla's scorn was open. 'I haven't put in years of hard study to end as a country G.P.'

'Oh,' Lucy said rather blankly. 'I should have thought that general practice would be interesting and—and very satisfying, Dr. Fielding.'

'Would you? But then you're not a doctor, are you, so you can't possibly know.' Camilla placed her empty cup on the tray. 'Thank you, Miss Grant, that was excellent coffee,' and she picked up the newspaper again.

'A dismissal,' thought Lucy, torn between annoyance and amusement as she walked back to the house. Caroline had a point! What could Mark see in the girl?

She began to understand over lunch, which Mark had asked if she could give them. Camilla had made no secret of her preference for going out, but her fiancé overruled her.

'I'm on call, darling. It would be better if we stayed in, if Lucy doesn't mind feeding us.'

He also insisted on eating with the family. Lucy served lunch in the dining-room, as the other couple were out for the day and there was plenty of room at the table. Mark was in an excellent humour, telling them that the repairs on the house were further on than he had realised. 'I called in on my way back from the hospital, and they've nearly finished the plastering. The stables need very little more doing to them, so you'll be able to have the horses there as soon as we move in.'

He exchanged a smile with his fiancée and Lucy saw Caroline grip her glass so tightly that her knuckles showed white. She had half expected her sister to go out for lunch, but Caroline had chosen to stay, and must be suffering savage pangs of jealousy.

Camilla returned Mark's smile. 'I'm glad of that, darling. I don't want to leave them at home longer than necessary.'

'Is it true you do show jumping, Dr Fielding?' asked Susan, her pretty face alive with interest, for like many young girls she was mad about horses.

Camilla's smile was gracious. She seemed to prefer Susan to the rest of the family. 'Yes, dear, but not very often nowadays—I haven't much time. But I hunt when I can, and I compete in the occasional point-to-point.'

'There's a well-known one near here,' Susan told her eagerly. 'It would be great if you entered for it.'

'Perhaps I will,' Camilla answered. She laid a hand on Mark's arm. 'You should too, darling, though you're a bit out of practice.'

'No time, my love,' Mark said goodhumouredly. 'But I hope to do some hunting next season.'

William stirred in his chair and opened his mouth to object, so Lucy rushed into the conversation before he could drop a brick. 'How many horses have you got, Dr Fielding?'

'Two,' said Camilla, 'and I'm looking after Mark's as well. Do you remember when we bought Starlight?' she asked, turning towards him.

By the end of the meal Lucy understood a good deal more

about the couple's relationship. They had known each other since childhood, for their parents were old friends. Mark had brought a couple of bottles of wine and they lingered over lunch, pleasantly relaxed with the exception of Caroline, who sat stiff and silent and pokerfaced.

Because he was on duty Mark had only one glass of wine, but he asked for a second cup of coffee. As he finished it he sighed contentedly and pushed back his chair. 'That was a splendid meal. Wasn't it, Camilla?'

'Very nice,' Camilla agreed, without much warmth. 'Shall we sit in the garden, darling?'

They rose from the table and Mark slipped an arm through hers. 'You'll have to get Lucy to give you some tips on cooking. Camilla hardly knows how to boil an egg,' he added, his smile indulgent.

Camilla looked decidedly put out at this masculine lack of tact. 'I've never had to,' she said shortly. 'But anyone can learn to cook. Just a question of following the directions carefully—not unlike a chemistry experiment, except that it needs less brains!'

'And that puts my little accomplishment where it belongs!' thought Lucy, wondering why Camilla seemed to feel such an urge to belittle her.

'Snooty bitch,' muttered Caroline, staring after them as they went down the hall. 'I suppose she'll expect full-time help in the house when she's married.'

'Surely that would be reasonable,' said Lucy, striving to be fair. 'She'll be a consultant herself before long, and if she's working full-time they'll need some sort of housekeeper.'

'I'm surprised Mark agrees to that sort of set-up.'

'Perhaps he hasn't much choice. If he wants to marry her he has to accept the fact that she's a dedicated career woman.'

There would be problems in their marriage, thought Lucy, for though she had grown to like Mark, she knew that he could be difficult, brusque and bad-tempered when things had gone wrong at the hospital, often impatient. However, Camilla had known him all her life. She must be aware of his less attractive side.

CHAPTER FIVE

In the end Camilla didn't leave on Monday. Lucy was busy over breakfast when the telephone rang, so Susan answered it. She came skipping into the dining-room to give Lucy a message.

'That was the woman who was supposed to be coming today. She wants to cancel because her mother's ill.'

Lucy put the toast on the table and a fresh pot of coffee. She remembered what she had told Camilla on Saturday, and wondered if the other girl did too. If Camilla had forgotten, Susan was quick to remind her.

'That's lucky, Camilla! Now you can stay on.'

'Dr Fielding,' Lucy said quickly, and Mark smiled.

'Rubbish, Lucy! Camilla doesn't expect you to be so formal.'

Susan pulled a face at her sister behind Mark's back and returned to the kitchen. Camilla poured coffee and said nothing.

'You'd like to stay, wouldn't you, darling?' asked Mark. 'Give you a chance to spend more time at the house.'

'Ye-es. But I could see it this morning and go back later.'

'You've got a few days' leave, so why not stay?' Mark asked quietly, and put his hand over hers. They stared at each other for a few moments, then Camilla smiled, with a sweetness that Lucy had never seen before. A smile that perhaps she kept for him alone.

'Of course, darling,' she said softly.

Lucy felt out of place, an intruder on an intimate little scene. She was moving quietly towards the door when Mark spoke to her. 'All right, Lucy? Camilla can have the room?' She nodded and he said briskly, 'So that's

75

settled, then.' He looked pleased at having got his own
way, and Lucy wished that Susan hadn't taken that telephone call. The prospect of having Camilla around for
another few days was not exactly a pleasant one.

On Tuesday Mark had a free afternoon, which had been
used by his predecessor for private practice. As a very new
consultant he had as yet no private patients, so he took the
opportunity to go over to the house with Camilla. They
were eating out that evening, but arrived back soon after
ten.

Lucy was sitting on the lawn, relaxing after an evening's
gardening. She felt hot, tired and grubby, so that when
Mark and Camilla came up to her she was acutely conscious
of her untidy appearance, which contrasted so strikingly
with theirs. Mark wore a light grey summer suit and a crisp
white shirt. Camilla was cool and attractive in a cream-
coloured dress. They looked smart and assured and very
pleased with themselves.

'Hallo, Lucy!' Mark stopped in front of the bench and
smiled down at her. 'You were right, the White Hart's
first-rate. We had a splendid meal, didn't we, Camilla?'

'Splendid,' Camilla agreed, sliding a hand through
Mark's arm and giving Lucy a faintly pitying look. 'Don't
you ever get out, Miss Grant?'

'Lucy,' said Mark. 'Why are you two always so formal?'

'All right then, Lucy. You can't have much fun, tied to
this place.' She eyed Lucy's soil-stained hands with disapproval. 'You'll ruin them if you don't wear gloves.'

'I can't work properly in gloves,' Lucy said sharply,
irritated by the other girl's patronising manner. She stood
up and tucked her shirt into her jeans. 'If you'll excuse
me——'

'Don't rush off,' Mark cut in. 'We've good news, Lucy.
The builder has named a date for when he expects to be
finished. So all that remains is to decide on our wedding
day!'

There was a curious tightness in Lucy's chest, and for a moment or two she couldn't speak. 'Good,' she managed, then feeling this wasn't enough, 'So when do you think it will be?'

'End of September or beginning of October,' Camilla smiled. 'Father will be on a lecture tour in the States, so we'll have to check on his dates first.'

'Let's have a celebration drink,' Mark suggested. 'I'll bring something out.'

'I don't think——' began Lucy.

'You look as if you need one,' he said firmly. 'Scotch and soda? Sherry? The usual for you, Camilla?'

He strode off in the direction of the house. Camilla brushed the bench with a well kept hand and sat down beside Lucy.

'Tell me a bit more about the house,' Lucy suggested, to break the rather awkward silence.

It was an old rectory, Camilla said, built in late Jacobean times, and unoccupied since the present rector had moved to a small modern house. Run down but with great potential. 'And when we come to sell it we should make a good profit.'

'When you come to ... but surely you won't want to move again if you both like it?'

'Of course we shall move, when Mark gets a better post.'

'But ... isn't he happy in *this* job?'

Camille explained, in that patronising way of hers, that a man of Mark's brilliance would scarcely be content to work in a dump like Barnslow General all his life.

'Then why did he come here if he despises it so much?' Lucy asked, annoyed by this scornful remark about her local hospital, which might not have the prestige of a major city hospital, but did sterling work just the same.

'Because he wanted to move up a grade, of course. He'd had enough of being a senior registrar. He wanted to run his own unit, and there's no post coming up at Queen's for a few years. But when there is'—Camilla smiled and smoothed her hair—'I shall persuade him to apply.'

'Might he need persuading?' asked Lucy.

'Mark has a sentimental idea about living in the country. He says he doesn't want his children to grow up in London. But I shall work on him when the time comes.' Camilla smiled again, very sure of her ability to talk her fiancé into her way of thinking.

Mark arrived back with their drinks on a small tray. 'You must come and see the house next time we're going there, Lucy.' He was full of enthusiasm, wanting to talk about it. Camilla, on the other hand, seemed to have had enough of the subject, was plainly bored by Mark's plans for the garden and whether they might have problems over the septic tank.

She wrinkled her elegant nose at him. 'Can't we leave that sort of thing to the builders?'

'Sanitation's important, darling. As a doctor you should know that.'

Camilla put down her empty glass and stood up. 'I'll leave you to it, then. I want to ring Mother.'

Mark watched his fiancée as she walked towards the house, his smile rueful. 'She isn't very interested in domestic matters,' he observed, 'but she'll learn.'

'I hope so,' said Lucy, then thinking this sounded ungracious, 'I mean, I'm sure she will. When I took over the running of this house I was pretty ignorant myself.'

'Were you?' Mark looked surprised. 'Somehow I'd have thought you were always a practical sort of girl.'

'Not always,' Lucy answered, and gave a little sigh for the carefree days when she had been as gay as young Susan was now. When her mother had had to chase her up to do her homework, and to reprove her gently for spending too much time with her boy-friends. 'I wasn't always dull and domesticated,' she added wryly, then felt ashamed of this exhibition of self-pity. 'Thanks for the drink,' she added abruptly, and followed Camilla into the house.

*

The following evening Lucy called in at Barnslow General to see how Caroline was doing. She was worried about her sister, who had looked increasingly strained over the week-end, and hadn't telephoned since. She found her in the residents' common-room with several of her colleagues.

Caroline registered surprise when Lucy walked in. 'I felt like a break from the house,' Lucy said casually.

'Couldn't you have found something more exciting to do?' Caroline retorted ungraciously. 'It's not a very good evening for a visit anyway. I'm pretty busy.'

She had not looked busy when Lucy arrived. She had been stretched out on a sofa, reading the *British Medical Journal*.

'If you like I'll do your night round,' Henry Wilson offered, but Caroline shook her head.

'Thanks, but there are one or two problems I must see myself.'

They sat for half an hour or so, then Caroline looked pointedly at her watch. 'I can see you want to get rid of me,' Lucy said quietly, and Caroline rose with alacrity.

'I do have to get on.'

Lucy followed her towards the door, and Caroline said irritably, 'You don't have to go. Henry will look after you.'

'I came to see you.'

Caroline went on walking. The residents had their own house in the hospital grounds. Her sister went out of the front door, with Lucy close behind.

'Do stop a moment,' begged Lucy. 'We've hardly had two words together.'

'What do you want to say?' snapped Caroline, and Lucy put a hand on her arm.

'I just want to know if you're all right.'

'Why shouldn't I be?'

'Because ... oh, Caro, you don't have to pretend with me. You look so unhappy.'

'Leave me alone, Lucy! Just leave me alone!' Caroline's voice rose and two nurses passing by stared at them curiously. She put a hand over her mouth to stifle a sob. When she had herself under control again she managed a wavering smile. 'I know you want to help, but you can't. Nobody can. How much longer is she staying?'

'She leaves tomorrow. The builders are making progress at last.'

'So when are they getting married?'

'Early autumn, probably. Can you come home tomorrow evening?'

'Maybe. I must go now.'

As Lucy walked to the bus stop she reflected that Caroline seemed to have accepted the inevitable, and no longer deluded herself that Mark and Camilla might break up. That was why she was so unhappy, but she would get over it in time, helped perhaps by Henry Wilson, who seemed just as devoted, judging by his behaviour this evening.

She arrived home to a family crisis, raised voices from the first floor, and Susan and William listening by the kitchen door. They looked shaken and upset and very relieved to see their older sister.

'What's going on?' asked Lucy, as she heard Camilla's clear voice, shriller than usual, and her father's gruff tones in reply.

'I don't know,' muttered Susan, and William said angrily, 'She's being beastly to Dad. She called him a thief!'

Lucy took the stairs two at a time and arrived at the door of Mark's sitting-room as her father was coming out, looking flushed and guilty. He wore his shabby old sweater and bedroom slippers. He looked unkempt and disreputable and his breath smelt of whisky.

'What are you doing, Dad?' Lucy gasped, but he pushed past her and stumbled upstairs without a word.

Camilla appeared in the doorway. Unlike Lucy's father she had plenty to say. 'I came back unexpectedly to find him at Mark's whisky. I've thought before now that it seemed to be going very fast. What an incredibly mean and petty thing to do!' She glared at poor Lucy, as if the other girl was responsible for her father's behaviour.

'Dr Fielding, please, please don't make a fuss.' Lucy looked anxiously towards the other rooms and Camilla gave an angry laugh.

'They're out. We were out too, but I came back early because Mark got an urgent call from the hospital. I caught him at it, gave him such a shock that he dropped the bottle.' She poked scornfully with her toe and the whisky bottle rolled under a table.

Lucy stared at the damp patch on the carpet. 'I'm very sorry.' She followed Camilla into the room and shut the door. 'My father ... you must see how it is ... he's getting too dependent on alcohol ...'

'You mean he's an alcoholic?' Camilla asked crisply, and Lucy nodded miserably.

'I suppose so. And he has so little money. He can't afford to buy much himself.'

'So you think that excuses him?'

'Of course not! I'm trying to explain. I'll buy another bottle.'

'I reckon you owe Mark a good deal more than one bottle,' Camilla stated unkindly. 'This wasn't the first time —he admitted as much.'

Humiliated and unhappy, Lucy repeated her apologies. 'I suppose you'll have to tell Mark?'

A foolish question. 'Of course I shall. If he has any sense he'll look for another place. He never intended to stay here originally. It was just a stopgap until he found something better.'

'I know,' said Lucy, her eyes on the carpet. 'But he likes it here.'

'Likes it? My dear girl, I hate to disillusion you, but he didn't stop because he likes it.' Camilla's smile was maddeningly superior.

'What are you trying to say?'

'He stayed because he felt sorry for you and your pathetic

attempts to make ends meet.'

'That's not true!' cried Lucy. 'He knew I could fill his rooms any time.'

'If you say so,' shrugged Camilla with evident disbelief.

Lucy felt she couldn't bear any more of this horrible conversation. 'I'll talk to Mark when he gets back,' she said, and went quickly from the room. She paused, irresolute, at the foot of the stairs that led to the second floor bedrooms. Should she go to her father? Not tonight. Tomorrow, when she felt calmer. Tonight, however, she must talk to Mark, if possible before Camilla did.

She went into the garden and hung around near the barn. When he drove in she hurried over to the car.

'Mark?'

In the gloom he mistook her for Camilla for a moment. 'Hallo, darling! Oh, it's you, Lucy.'

'Mark, I must speak to you.' She blurted out the sordid little story and Mark listened in silence.

'I see. Don't look so upset, my dear. No one could possibly blame you.'

'But I feel responsible. I should have guessed what was happening.'

'Rubbish!' Mark was at his most positive. 'No way that you could.'

'Camilla blames me.'

'I'm sure she wouldn't be so foolish.' He put a comforting arm round her shoulders and they moved towards the house.

'I'll pay you back for what he took,' she promised.

'Mmmm?' He stared down at her. 'For God's sake, Lucy, the whisky isn't important. It's why he did it that matters.'

As they went in at the front door Camilla came downstairs, her expression sharpening as she saw her fiancé's arm around Lucy. 'Getting your story in first?' she asked caustically, and Mark stared at her in surprise.

'That was unkind, darling. Poor Lucy is very upset.'

'So she should be! I wouldn't care to have a father who's a thief.'

'Stop it, Camilla! What in God's name has got into you?' Mark sounded really angry and Camilla looked taken aback. 'Mr Grant may need treatment,' he continued more quietly. 'We'll talk about it tomorrow.'

'We?' asked Camilla. 'What has it got to do with us?'

Mark's mouth compressed and his eyes were cold as he looked at his fiancée. 'He needs help, as you ought to know. You've done a stint in psychiatry, like all of us.'

'I'm not interested in psychiatry.'

'Nor am I, but I'm interested in people.' He gave Lucy a reassuring squeeze, let go of her and marched Camilla back upstairs, his expression grim.

He was being exceptionally kind and understanding. The tears that Lucy had held in check until now began to flow. She went into the kitchen, was relieved to find it empty, and subsided into her favourite chair.

Next morning Mark came down to breakfast on his own. He said very little, but when he was about to leave he took her aside and spoke in a low, earnest voice.

'Are you on good terms with your G.P.? You should have a chat with him about your father.'

Their old G.P., whom Lucy had known all her life, had recently retired. His replacement was young, and Lucy doubted if he would be very sympathetic to the problems of a middle-aged man without a job. When she said this Mark frowned.

'You can't possibly know that. It's his job to help your father. Alcoholism is a disease and has to be treated as such. If your G.P. can't cope he should refer him to a psychiatrist. Go and see him as a first step, or better still persuade your father to go. And go with him if he'll allow you to.'

At her doubtful look he added impatiently that in his opinion it was a matter of urgency. 'Your father doesn't strike me as the sort of man who would filch from other people unless he was desperate.

They were standing by the open front door and the sun was streaming in. It was a beautiful day, but Lucy's heart felt heavy. 'I'll do my best, Mark. And ... thanks for being so kind.'

He was already moving, but he hung on his heel for a moment. 'I hope you won't be too critical of Camilla. This sort of thing is outside her experience, and she hasn't much imagination.'

'What was that about me?'

They both glanced up, to see Camilla at the top of the stairs, striking in a blue silk caftan. Mark ignored her question. 'You look very fetching, darling! I'm sorry I couldn't wait breakfast for you, but I have a clinic at nine.'

Camilla descended the stairs with the assurance of a model girl. 'I overslept, but I thought if I didn't waste time dressing, I might just catch you.' She leant towards Mark and kissed him on the cheek; she was a tall girl and hardly had to reach up to him. 'See you at lunchtime, darling.'

'Right! If I'm late wait in my office. I've quite a few problems to sort out.'

When he had gone Camilla drifted into the dining-room. 'Coffee and a grapefruit, please. Nothing else.'

The eight o'clock news was on when Lucy returned with the tray, and the other visitors were not down yet.

'Mark says I owe you an apology,' drawled Camilla, fixing Lucy with her large blue eyes. 'He thinks I was unsympathetic last night.'

'That's all right,' mumbled Lucy, embarrassed and longing to get away.

'So we'll forget about it, shall we? No hard feelings?'

'No, of course not,' though some of her words would be difficult to forget. The thought that Mark had only stayed on because he was sorry for them rankled unpleasantly.

'What was Mark saying about me?' Camilla asked. 'Just before I came down?'

'Nothing really. Just that what happened last night wasn't—wasn't the sort of thing you're used to.'

Camilla stared for a moment, then laughed. 'Too true! No one in my family has to go around pinching other people's booze!'

An angry flush burned on Lucy's cheeks. 'Mark would never say a thing like that!'

'Mark's a man,' Camilla said meaningly. 'He's fallen for the brave little woman act you turn on so convincingly.'

Lucy was not a girl who ever posed, and she had always despised people who did so. Camilla's words stung, as they were doubtless intended to do. 'Why do you dislike me so much, Dr Fielding?' she asked quietly.

Camilla shrugged her indifference. 'I neither like nor dislike you, my dear girl. I hardly know you, after all.' As Lucy went out of the door she called after her, 'Mark will be settling my bill, so you can add it to his.'

Mark came back from the hospital very late, because it was his night on duty. He looked tired and irritable, but he insisted on talking to Lucy about her father.

'Come up to my room. I don't want to be interrupted.' He waved her into a chair and threw himself into the one opposite. 'Well? Have you fixed an appointment with his G.P.?' She shook her head. 'Why not?' he snapped.

'Dad won't agree that he needs any help.'

'Then the man's an idiot,' Mark said tersely. '*I'll* talk to him,' and he half rose from his chair.

'No!' At her exclamation he sat back again. 'I'll try again tomorrow. Dad's very sensitive, and you're not in the best of moods tonight.' He frowned, and she hurried on. 'Please don't think I'm ungrateful, but this is a family affair and—and——'

'You think I'm interfering?'

'No, of course I don't. But you look as if you've had a packet at work. It's not fair to involve you when you're so busy.'

'That's what Camilla said,' growled Mark. 'I told her I was involved.'

'Which I'm sure didn't please her.' Because she was tired herself Lucy spoke unwisely.'

Mark rose and crossed to her side, his expression forbidding, grey eyes narrowed as he stared down at her. 'Has that remark got any special meaning?' His voice was cool.

Flustered, Lucy looked back at him. 'I only meant— Camilla doesn't approve of your being friendly with me— with us,' she amended quickly, and flushed under his steady gaze.

'You had it right the first time,' he said drily. 'It's you, my dear Lucy, not your family, of whom she disapproves.' His mouth compressed, then he spoke again. 'Women are so unreasonable. What do I have to do to convince her I'm in love with her? We're engaged, for God's sake! We're getting married in the autumn.' He shoved his hands in his pockets and strode over to the window. With his back to her he spoke again. 'She's being unreasonable and absurdly possessive, but for the sake of peace perhaps I'd better move into a hotel. I hope you understand?' He hunched his broad shoulders and stared down at the garden.

His words came as an unpleasant shock to Lucy. 'But ... Camilla has no reason to be ... jealous?' The word came out hesitantly with a hint of a query.

Mark swung round angrily, startling her by the violence of his reaction. 'I've told her that! My God, I've told her that a dozen times! The idea is totally ridiculous.' He swept the thought away with a contemptuous gesture. 'But for some reason she's never liked my being here.' He returned to his chair and raised a hand to his forehead. 'We had a hell of a row before she left,' he said wearily. 'It's so unlike Camilla to lose her cool.'

'Then of course you must leave,' Lucy agreed. 'I'm very sorry that I've been the cause of trouble between you.'

He didn't look up. 'We'll talk about it tomorrow. And don't forget, keep on at your father.'

As she slipped from the room, Lucy saw Mark bang his fist on the arm of the chair in anger and frustration.

'Women!' he muttered under his breath, and then she closed the door on him and went downstairs.

CHAPTER SIX

'WHAT'S wrong, Lucy?' asked William, as his sister came into the kitchen.

Her father, hunched in his chair before the television, looked up quickly, then away again.

'Mark's leaving,' Lucy said bleakly. 'At the end of the week, I expect.'

They all looked astonished. 'But why?' cried Susan. 'I thought he was staying until his house is ready.'

'That may be weeks.' Lucy took the spare chair, rested her head against its back and closed her eyes. 'I don't want to talk about it now.'

Perhaps Mark might change his mind—persuade Camilla to be sensible, convince her that there was no need for jealousy. That the idea was, as he had just said, 'Totally ridiculous,' to be dismissed with a scornful gesture. He would never ever see Lucy as anyone but a girl he rather liked, and whom he also pitied, if Camilla was to be believed. He might perhaps be a little sorry to leave, because he was comfortable and settled, and got on well with them all.

Lucy would be bereft. She understood now, contemplating his departure, what she had come to feel for Mark. She loved him, though she knew it was hopeless. She understood now how Caroline felt, though unlike Caroline she would not indulge in fantasies. In a few months Mark would be married and living with Camilla in their new house. They would make a handsome and successful couple, an asset to the social life of the district. Young Mrs Franklin would be admired and envied. When Camilla was ready they would have children.

For the first time in her life Lucy knew the savage pain

of jealousy. She pressed her hands to her aching eyes and fought for self-control.

'Aren't you feeling well?' her father asked, coming out of his self-absorption to stare anxiously at his daughter.

'I've got a beastly headache, Dad. I think I'll go to bed.'

The headache wasn't an excuse. She took a couple of aspirins and in time it departed, leaving her without pain, but unable to sleep.

'You look flaked out,' Mark commented next morning, when she brought him his breakfast.

'I am a little tired,' she admitted with studied casualness. 'Have you decided when you'll be leaving?'

She wished that he wouldn't stare at her so fixedly, that someone else would come down to breakfast. 'I haven't thought about it,' he said shortly.

'Then I'd be grateful if you would. We can't afford to have two rooms empty.'

'I shan't leave without warning,' Mark answered irritably.

'At the weekend? Saturday morning? Then I can get the rooms ready for someone else to move in on Monday.'

'Anxious to get rid of me, my dear?' He made a joke of it, but she could see that he was put out. 'It's so damn silly! I've half a mind to stay on, and to hell with Camilla's idiotic notions.'

'I don't think that would be a good idea,' Lucy said steadily. 'I would rather you went, Mark.' He looked at her quickly, surprise and something else on his face. 'If you stay there'll only be more unpleasantness.' And if he stayed she would only fall more deeply, more hopelessly in love. 'I should be grateful if you would leave at the weekend,' Lucy said firmly, and walked out of the room before he could reply.

That Mark was offended he made very plain. He became once more the brusque stranger he had been on first acquaintance, to Lucy at any rate, for he was pleasant enough to the rest of the family. He was leaving on Sunday afternoon. When Lucy dusted his rooms on the Saturday, most of his possessions were packed, and some he had already taken away. The photograph of Camilla still stood on his bed table, where he could look at it last thing at night.

Lucy kept out of his way as much as she could, but on Sunday morning, when she was picking the first peas of the year, he came into the vegetable garden, accompanied by William and Susan.

Her brother had his camera in one hand. 'We're taking pictures, Luce. We want some of Mark with us all.'

'I'm busy, William. Take them without me.'

'Oh, come on, Lucy!' exclaimed Susan. 'Don't be a spoilsport! Even Dad's taking part,' and she caught her sister by the hand.

'I'm not dressed properly,' Lucy protested, looking down at her faded jeans and her old blue checked shirt.

'Doesn't matter!' William said scornfully, as she put a hand to her hair.

'What a vain girl you are!' Mark spoke for the first time, mocking and unfriendly. 'Just a few snapshots as a memento—you don't need to doll up for that.'

So they grouped themselves near the front door, Mr Grant and Lucy on the wooden bench, Susan and William behind. Then Mark joined them and William took over the camera.

'You'd look better all standing. Move closer. You're half out of the picture, Lucy.'

'Is she in it now?' asked Mark, putting an arm round her shoulders and drawing her into the group. She stiffened at his touch, stopped breathing for a few seconds and then let out a long sigh. Mark's hand was clamped firmly on her upper arm, while William fussed away with his exposure meter.

'Hurry up, Billy! I can't keep smiling for ever!' said young Susan.

'Some people don't seem able to smile at all,' drawled

Mark, slanting a glance at Lucy.

'Keep still!' yelled William. 'Look this way, please!' He clicked away several times before he allowed them to break up.

'I hope they turn out all right,' Susan remarked. 'I do wish you weren't leaving.'

Mark said pleasantly that of course he was sorry to be going, but it would be more convenient living closer to his new house. He would be staying in a small hotel in the same village. He could keep more of an eye on the builders, make a start on the garden on his evenings off.

'You could have done that from here,' Susan said disconsolately.

'You are staying for lunch?' asked William, and Mark nodded, his eyes on Lucy's downcast face.

'I should like to.'

'Oh, good. How soon, Luce? I'm absolutely famished!'

'Then you shouldn't have interrupted me,' Lucy pointed out, and went back to the vegetable garden. Mark joined her a minute or two later. 'I can manage,' she said stiffly, as he started to pluck the pea-pods.

He dropped a handful into her basket. 'Do you want me to go before lunch?' he asked abruptly, and hot colour flooded into her cheeks.

'Of course not. Susan and William would be terribly disappointed.'

'And you, Lucy? Perhaps you would be relieved?'

They were very close to each other, screened from the house by the thick hedge of pea plants. Lucy stared at Mark's sports shirt, open at the neck to expose his strong tanned throat. She ached with love for him, longed quite desperately to put out a hand and stroke his smooth brown skin. The midday sun beat down hotly. She felt lightheaded and in grave danger of losing her self-control.

'Why ever should I be relieved, Mark?' She stepped back from him and looked up challengingly.

He came towards her, mouth compressed in that familiar

way, an angry glitter in his eyes. 'Oh, God, I don't know,' he said savagely. 'I've given up trying to understand the female mind.'

'Then try this for an idea,' Lucy suggested, her voice beginning to rise. 'I don't care for Camilla's insinuations, and I don't care to be patronised. I was stupid enough to think you stayed on here because you liked it, not because you felt sorry for us.'

His look was one of total incomprehension. 'What are you talking about?' His hand shot out and caught her by the wrist. 'Come on, Lucy, what did that mean?'

When her eyes filled with humiliating tears, he swore softly and let her go. Lucy turned her back on him and went on picking peas, but clumsily because she couldn't see properly.

'Just for the record,' Mark said quietly, from somewhere close behind her, 'you couldn't be more wrong. I stayed because I liked it here. I shall miss you all, even you, bad-tempered little Lucy.'

Lunch was less of an ordeal than Lucy had expected. She was busy carving, serving, keeping an eye on the next course, so she didn't have to take much part in the conversation.

At the end of the meal Mark leant back in his chair. 'I've been spoilt by your cooking, Lucy, though they say the Crown's not at all bad. You must all come and eat with me there one weekend.'

'Super!' cried Susan, her face lighting up.

'And see your house again?' William asked hopefully.

Mark smiled at them both. 'Why not? We'll make a definite date when I've looked at the duty roster.'

Later they all accompanied him out to the car. Before he got in he shook Mr Grant's hand and said quietly, 'You should get that appointment any day,' smiled in a general way at the rest of them and was off.

Lucy stared after the car and fought for self-control.

There were long hours to get through before she could seek the sanctuary of her bedroom.

'What did he mean, Dad? What appointment?' asked William.

Their father's pasty face was momentarily tinged with colour. 'An appointment at the hospital, son.' He fell behind the youngsters for a word with Lucy. 'It's my fault he's left, isn't it? It's because of what happened that night?'

It was the first time he had referred to the incident of the whisky. 'No, Dad, that had nothing to do with it,' Lucy said sadly. 'His fiancée wanted him to move.'

Mr Grant sat down heavily on the bench near the front door. 'A snobbish young woman. Your mother wouldn't have liked her.'

She joined him. 'You didn't tell me you'd been to the doctor.'

He smiled faintly. 'Mark took me yesterday morning— kept on at me until I gave way. It wasn't as bad as I expected. The new G.P. was quite decent.'

'Mark took you?' She wondered why he hadn't mentioned it, then realised that they had scarcely been speaking to each other. How kind of him to have bothered. She herself had been so wrapped up in her own affairs that she had forgotten all about it. 'Who are you seeing at the hospital?'

Her father, looking uncomfortable, admitted that it was the senior psychiatrist. 'They say he's very good on—on drink problems.' He avoided her eyes. 'Mark has been extraordinarily decent about everything. Ah well, it's a relief to know he isn't leaving on my account.'

If Caroline minded Mark's departure she gave very little sign of it. She was working very hard because this was the holiday season, and with some of their colleagues away the remaining residents had extra duties to perform. Lucy wondered if the same applied to Mark, though he always seemed to carry such a heavy work load, he could hardly be expected to take on much more. She wondered if he was lonely in the impersonal atmosphere of a hotel, though for all she knew Camilla might be staying there frequently on her off duty nights. She wondered if anyone kept Mark's supper hot when he worked late at the hospital, as she had always done, if anyone made him a hot drink last thing at night.

She spent far too much time thinking about him, however hard she tried not to do so. Then one day when she was in Barnslow, doing her main shopping of the week, she met him in the bank. As she pushed open the swing doors and wheeled her shopping basket in, her heart gave a thump and she came to a sudden halt.

Mark was at the counter, writing a cheque. She moved quickly past him to the far end of the bank, hoping he hadn't noticed her, stared hard at a notice without taking in what it said, and waited her turn with the cashier. As she put the wad of notes in her handbag she cast a casual glance along the counter, and was relieved to see that he had gone. She emerged from the cool of the bank into bright sunlight, blinking in the glare. Someone touched her on the arm. Mark was waiting by the door.

She simulated surprise. 'Why, hallo! Fancy meeting you!'

'You saw me inside,' he said drily, 'though you pretended you didn't. I wish I knew what I've done to upset you. You surely don't blame me for Camilla's behaviour?'

She found it difficult to act naturally. It was two weeks since he had left, and there was scarcely a waking hour when she hadn't thought about him.

He glanced at his watch. 'I've nothing at the hospital till midday. Come and have coffee with me.'

'I don't think——'

'I do.' He hooked a hand through her arm and guided her purposefully along the crowded pavement. Mark at his most determined, she thought, beginning to smile in spite of herself. He smiled back at her, and any doubts were swept away in a wave of pure happiness, because she was with him again.

They found a quiet café down a narrow alley, with white walls and dark panelling. Mark sat with his back to the window and studied her critically.

'You're not looking very fit. Working too hard, I suppose.'

He asked about her father and Lucy told him that the hospital appointment wasn't until next week, though their G.P. was keeping an eye on him. About William and Susan. Lucy said that they were fine. Into the little silence that descended on them Lucy put her own question.

'Have you . . . fixed a date for the wedding yet?'

He didn't answer at once. He stirred his coffee and his brows drew together. 'Camilla wants to put off the decision. They've offered her a post as acting consultant at Q.C.H. Maybe three months, maybe six. One of their anaesthetists has gone off with a relief team to that place in South America where they had the earthquake.'

A faint hope stirred in Lucy, to be instantly suppressed. If Mark got tired of waiting there was no reason why he should turn to her. 'Couldn't she have found a locum nearer to Barnslow?' she asked.

'It wouldn't be the same. A stint as acting consultant at Queen's will give her a head start when she's applying for permanent posts.'

'But the house will be ready quite soon, won't it?'

'I know,' he said heavily, 'so I shall move in on my own.' He sounded thoroughly fed up and Lucy felt very sorry for him.

'Isn't there any chance that she may turn it down?'

'You know Camilla,' he said flatly. 'And backed up by her family she'll do what's best for her career.' His mouth twisted. 'You can't expect darling Camilla to throw away a chance like this,' he added in a high affected voice, that made several people turn to stare at him.

Lucy started to laugh and he joined in, but without

genuine humour. 'Does Camilla's mother really talk like that?' she asked.

'Worse,' he said gloomily. 'They say if you want to know what a girl will be like at fifty, study her mother.'

That didn't sound very loving, but if Camilla was being difficult it might explain the hard edge to his manner, which she had noticed the moment they had met. 'Oh, Mark, I'm so sorry.' She wasn't being hypocritical, for she loved him enough to want his happiness. 'She might still change her mind.'

'Not Camilla.'

'But when she's a consultant she'll have more free time than she does as a registrar, won't she?'

'Oh, sure, but I'm getting a bit tired of dashing up and down to London.'

'I should have thought,' Lucy said carefully, 'that she would want to come down here.' She was silent, trying to work something out. 'Mark, if—if she's inclined to be jealous of other girls you meet, then I just don't understand her attitude over this.'

'She isn't usually jealous,' said Mark. 'She knows she has no reason to be.'

'But then——'

'But in your case it was different.' She felt her colour begin to rise and put her hands up to her cheeks. Mark looked at her steadily. 'However, she doesn't see you as a threat any more, now I'm no longer living in your house.' There was something disagreeable about his expression, a sort of cynical amusement that made Lucy feel uncomfortable.

'I don't think she would like our having coffee together,' she said unhappily.

Mark banged the table with the flat of his hand, his face taut with anger. 'I'll meet whom I bloody well please!' At her startled expression his face softened and he leant forward, to say quietly, 'Sorry, Lucy, I'm a bit on edge at present.' He looked at his watch, said regretfully that he would have liked to stay longer, but he was seeing a patient at twelve.

On the pavement outside the café he took her hand in his and gave it a firm squeeze. 'I'm glad we met. And I haven't forgotten about that dinner date. I've been doing extra weekend duty because of the holiday roster.' He let her hand go, then paused as if struck by a sudden thought. 'I'm free on Wednesday evening. Why don't you come over to see the house?'

'All of us, you mean?'

'Just you. I'd value your advice on one or two problems.'

'Camilla can't decide?' she queried.

'She isn't likely to be down for a week or two,' he said shortly. 'Please come. You have a real flair for making houses attractive.'

Lucy knew that she would get no pleasure out of looking round the house where Mark would be living some day with Camilla. She ought to make some excuse, say she was too busy. Instead she weakened and said that she would like that. She loved seeing round old houses.

Mark looked pleased. 'I'll pick you up at seven, then. We can eat somewhere on the way.'

Tempting though the idea was she had to refuse. 'I have to serve an evening meal, remember. Pick me up at eight. Or why don't you eat with us? The others would like that.'

It ended with a visit from the whole family, even her father deciding to go. Lucy fell in love with the place on sight, and was astounded that Camilla wasn't longing to move in at the first opportunity. It was a beautifully proportioned house, shabby but without a trace of damp. Its mellow brick walls were a riot of climbing roses, red and yellow and apricot. At the rear were the stables and a cluster of outbuildings, and beyond these the paddocks where Camilla would keep her horses.

The builders' equipment was everywhere—ladders, sacks of cement, plasterboard, giant cans of emulsion paint.

'It's so beautiful as it is,' said Lucy, standing in the

middle of the drawing-room, which opened on to the rose garden. 'I hope you won't modernise it too much, destroy all its character.'

'Not if I have anything to do with it,' Mark said decisively. 'I'm glad you like it.'

'Like it? I absolutely love it! It's the only house I've been in that I've liked better than our own!'

He smiled faintly. 'Pity Camilla doesn't share your enthusiasm.'

She stared at him. 'She does want to live here? You didn't talk her into buying an old house against her judgment?'

'Oh, she likes it well enough,' he shrugged, 'but she's not prepared to devote much time to it. She'd be quite happy to employ an interior decorator—leave it all in his hands— end up with a beautiful show place. That's not what I want.'

Susan and William were thundering about overhead, their footsteps loud on the bare boards, and Mr Grant was exploring the stables. They were alone on the ground floor, and Lucy was too conscious of Mark's closeness. 'Can I see round the garden?' she asked brightly, and moved towards the door.

'Later. I haven't shown you upstairs yet.'

'I'd rather see the garden, before it gets dark.'

Her breath coming faster than usual, she opened the door on to the terrace. Mark reached across her and shut it again. 'It'll be light for ages. We'll go upstairs now.'

The main staircase curved gently upwards, with a wide half landing lit by tall windows. Lucy could imagine a bowl of roses there. She paused to admire the view, but Mark had gone ahead to throw open a door on to a large and lovely bedroom.

This was where they would sleep when they were married. Before they were married, probably, for Camilla had made it very plain that they were already lovers. She must never come here again. Never! It was tearing her to pieces, thinking of Mark and Camilla making love in this beautiful room.

'It's ... very attractive,' she said inadequately, and walked out on to the landing.

Mark followed her more slowly, and opened another door on to a smaller room. Later, as they walked down the stone steps that led to the rose garden, he asked about her father.

'He saw the psychiatrist this morning, and I think he liked him, though he's not keen to discuss it.'

'Is he going to be an in-patient?'

'I don't think so. You do notice an improvement, even after one visit?'

He smiled down at her earnest young face. 'Yes, I do. I expect the G.P. has helped too. Perhaps that's why you're looking more relaxed yourself. Or is it because I've gone?' Her heart jolted oddly, and she stared up at him, her mouth a little open, unable to answer. 'Joke,' he said mildly, took her by the arm and led her towards an arch-way that gave on to the main lawn. 'You were rather anxious to get rid of me,' he reminded her. 'In fact you asked me to go.'

This was dangerous ground, to be trodden with care. 'Only because I was so fed up,' Lucy explained. 'But not with you,' she added hastily.

'With Camilla, you mean?'

'Well ...' Camilla was the girl he loved. She didn't want to upset him.

Mark gave her an odd sort of smile, then sat down on a stone bench set into a recess, in the thick yew hedge. 'I know how bloody-minded Camilla can be.' She gaped at him, and he went on steadily, 'She's spoilt and wilful, an awful snob, not very sensitive to other people's feelings.'

'And yet you're in love with her.' What an idiotic thing to say! 'I mean,' Lucy rushed on, 'she must have lots of good qualities, or you wouldn't love her. Would you?' she ended, her voice very low.

'Let's say I love her in spite of her faults,' Mark amended wryly. 'And having plenty of my own'—he caught her eye and they both began to laugh—'Having a fair share of faults myself,' he ended with a grin, 'I'm reasonably tolerant of hers.' When she said nothing he went on, 'I'm used to them, after all. We grew up together. I used to take her riding when she was a little girl, kiss her better when she fell off her horse! Not that it often happened.' He was talking more to himself than to her, Lucy realised. He was leaning forward, elbows on knees, fingers laced under his chin, and she studied the strong planes of his face. His crisp dark hair was cut shorter than the current fashion, but it suited him. Camilla must be mad, she thought. He was an extremely attractive man and he was surrounded by young women, some of whom would not hesitate to encourage him. The less scrupulous girls would certainly not allow his engagement to deter them. It might even act as a challenge.

'There still seems a lot to do in the house,' she remarked. 'Will it be ready when they promised?'

Mark's mouth turned down. 'They keep finding something else to do, but I'm fed up with hotel life. I'm moving in on July the first, even if I can only use two rooms.'

'If you're on your own it won't matter.'

'Camilla will be coming down at weekends,' he reminded her. Lucy was silent, digesting that, and he rubbed his forehead as if he was tired or dispirited. 'If only she would compromise over a job,' he went on.

'You miss her very much, don't you, Mark?' Lucy asked quietly.

He let out a long sigh. 'Yes, I do. And the thought of a winter here on my own isn't particularly appealing. I'm not a man who makes friends quickly.'

That admission touched Lucy, for she had always thought of Mark as entirely self-sufficient, the sort of man who would never admit to the ordinary human weaknesses of loneliness and despondency.

'You do have friends, Mark,' and when he stared at her

she added shyly, 'At least I hope you think of us as friends.'

He smiled warmly. 'You're a sweet girl, Lucy. And a good listener.' The smile became rueful. 'You make a man say more than he means to. I don't usually bore other people with my problems.'

'I wasn't bored—honestly.' A little breeze blew her hair across her face. Mark leant forward and smoothed it back, an unimportant gesture, a mild show of affection, of gratitude even, because she had let him unburden himself. She was very conscious of their isolation, tucked away in this quiet corner of the garden. At the bottom of the lawn there was a clump of silver birches and beyond lay open fields. A blackbird flew low in front of them, giving its evening call, clear and bell-like.

Lucy would have been happy to go on sitting there with Mark, letting him talk about his affairs, enjoying the peaceful and beauiful scene, but she knew it was unwise, that it had been a bad idea to walk round the garden with him—something not to be repeated if she valued her peace of mind.

'Shall we move on?' she suggested. 'The others must be wondering where we are.'

CHAPTER SEVEN

ON Saturday week there was a fête at Barnslow General Hospital, and Lucy, whose mother had been one of the chief organisers in the old days, was always pressed into helping on a stall. She did so willingly, and this year there was the added bonus that she might meet Mark. Most of the consultants turned up, spent a few pounds and gossiped together in the way that medical men do, talking shop even when they are off duty.

Lucy was helping Mrs Girling, an old friend of her mother's, to run the cake stall. Mrs Girling, ample in a blue silk dress that did nothing for her high colour, fussed around the front of the stall, rearranging the cakes, and flicking a plump hand at the clustering flies.

'Silly of people not to wrap them in polythene. But we've a good batch this year, my dear. They should make a lot of money.'

Henry Wilson came up to the stall, and with him the house physician who had entertained Lucy at the last hospital party.

'Hallo, boys!' breezed Mrs Girling. 'I'm sure you'd like to supplement your hospital tea with a nice cake. Is the food as bad as ever?' for Mrs Girling's eldest son had worked as a houseman at Barnslow the year before.

The house physician, whose name Lucy had forgotten, chose a chocolate cake.

'That'll be seventy pence, Dr ...?'

'Stevens. Chris Stevens.' The young man had a nice smile. 'How about sampling some of this when you've finished here?' His gaze was openly admiring, lingering on Lucy's smooth brown legs and on the shining fall of her long brown hair.

Lucy felt warmed by his interest, and smiled back at him. 'I'd like that. Thanks.'

'See you in the mess, then,' said Chris, and wandered off in the direction of the hoop-la stall.

'You young things are so casual nowadays,' observed Mrs Girling. 'What a way to ask a girl for a date!'

'Hardly a date, Mrs Girling. Just tea in the residents' mess.'

Mrs Girling gave her a nudge. 'It won't end in the residents' mess, my dear! *I* saw the way he was looking at you,' and then to Lucy's relief several people approached, so that the two of them were busy selling their wares.

The afternoon sun was hot enough to melt the icing on the cakes. Lucy fiddled with the striped canvas awning, trying to pull it lower to give more shade. She was perched precariously on a slatted chair, tugging at a cord, when a familiar voice spoke behind her.

'You don't look very safe up there. Get down and I'll have a go.' Mark! She swung round eagerly, her face alight. Her foot slipped and she would have fallen, if he hadn't caught her.

'I'm sorry!' she gasped, as he held her for a moment until she had regained her balance. 'Can I sell you a cake, Mark?'

He took his hands away, and she wished he hadn't. 'We could do with one, couldn't we, Camilla?'

Lucy's eyes had been only for him, so that she hadn't noticed his companion. Now she looked at Camilla a little warily, hoping the other girl hadn't noticed her joy at meeting Mark. Camilla's face gave nothing away. She was, as always, cool and self-assured, and made Lucy, in her pretty peasant dress, feel lacking in style and sophistication.

'I'll take that one.' Camilla pointed to a coffee cake. She spoke to Mrs Girling, ignoring Lucy completely.

Mark, busy adjusting the awning, seemed unaware of any tension.

'You see to it, Lucy dear. I'm in a muddle over my

change,' Mrs Girling, looking flustered, retreated into the background.'

'Are you down for the weekend, Dr Fielding?' Lucy asked, for something to say.

The older girl nodded. 'Today and tomorrow. It's a pity we had to waste the afternoon coming here.'

Her glance roved over the noisy and colourful scene, for hospital fêtes were always well attended. A sticky small boy ran past, shouting at his companion, face smeared with ice cream, and Camilla's expression grew disdainful as she eyed the child's mother, vainly trying to control him.

'What a mob! Hurry up, darling, and let's get away. You've done your duty, for heaven's sake,' and she almost snatched the cake from Lucy's hands.

Mark finished fixing the awning and turned to his fiancée, looking faintly irritated. 'I've already told you, Camilla, that I promised to cover for McFee until five o'clock, so there's no point dashing off.'

'I don't see why you had to agree to do it this weekend,' Camilla grumbled, slipping a hand through his arm, as if to hurry him away.

'Because McFee is making some sort of speech to end the fête,' Mark retorted. 'I told you that already, but you weren't listening.' He smiled as he spoke, as if to take the sting out of his words, but the smile was a sharp one, and so was Camilla's in return.

Lucy had the impression that they were on the brink of a quarrel, that their weekend wasn't the joyful reunion that it should have been. As they walked off arm in arm, Mrs Girling raised her head from her accounts to watch them go.

'Good-looking pair. Who are they, my dear?' and when Lucy explained her expression grew thoughtful. 'So that's the new surgeon! They do say he's absolutely brilliant. What does Caro think of him?'

'She ... admires him too. She thinks we're lucky to have got him.' Mark and Camilla had disappeared into the crowd now. Why were they so edgy with one another? And why was Mark looking so tense and frustrated?

'Brilliant he may be,' commented Mrs Girling, 'but that young man has a very hard face! And as for his fiancée ...' Her voice tailed off as another customer approached.

The cake stall sold out before any of the others. 'Off you go, my dear,' Mrs Girling ordered benignly, 'and don't keep your admirer waiting!'

Tea had already been served when Lucy arrived in the residents' dining-room, but there were only a scattering of people at the big table in the window—Henry and Chris at one end, then a couple of women doctors, and at the far end, sitting on their own, Mark and Camilla. Mark was deep in conversation with his fiancée, as Lucy passed behind his chair to join the two young men.

'Where's Caroline?' she asked.

'Clerking a new admission,' said Henry. 'She should be down soon.'

Caroline hadn't been home for a week or so, and when she had come she had steered clear of intimate conversation. She had thrown out a few casual remarks about Henry, which Lucy had thought encouraging, and now here was Henry suggesting that he and Caro, Chris and she should make up a foursome on their next free evening. Lucy hesitated, wondering if Chris was being pushed into an outing he didn't really want.

'Wouldn't you and Caroline rather go on your own?' she asked Henry, but he grinned and shook his head.

'I'm not sure she wants a whole evening of my company. Be a sport, Lucy, here's Chris longing for you to say yes.'

That young man, blushing ingenuously, added a shy agreement, that he very much wanted Lucy to come with them. He was rather sweet, she thought, feeling positively motherly towards him, though in fact he must have been at least as old as she was.

The other residents left and Caroline joined them, throwing one sharp glance in Camilla's direction, and then turning deliberately, so that she looked away from the couple at the end of the table. Lucy studied her sister and decided that she looked much better.

The chocolate cake was cut and everyone agreed that it was an improvement on hospital fare. 'Would you like a piece, sir?' Henry asked, waving the plate in Mark's direction.

He smiled and nodded, coming down to their end of the table to take some. Chris, looking very young and earnest, was telling Lucy what a marvellous nurse she would have made. 'Honestly! The patients would love you. You have such a sympathetic face.'

Lucy was acutely aware of Mark, bending forward directly opposite, helping himself to cake. As he straightened he stared at Chris for a moment, mouth quirking, as if he found him rather comical. She jumped up, saying that she wanted more tea. The urn stood on a side table, and as he passed by her Mark paused for a moment, a gleam of mockery in his dark eyes.

'Be kind to the lad,' he murmured. 'Be *sympathetic,* Lucy.'

'Oh, go away,' she hissed. 'I think he's very sweet.'

'Sweet?' Mark queried, with lifted eyebrows. 'I should call him thoroughly wet,' and with this unkind remark he left her.

Lucy was furious with him, both for laughing at her and for putting into words what she had begun to feel. 'Wet' wasn't a bad description for poor Chris. He was nice but uninspiring, young for his age in spite of his qualifications. Caroline told her later that he was very clever, 'Though he's not too good at handling patients.'

'I should have thought that was rather a disadvantage in a doctor,' Lucy said with unusual tartness, for she was already regretting the proposed evening out. Half an hour of Chris's company had been more than enough; a whole evening could be dreary in the extreme.

However, she had agreed to go and there was no way

out of it, without giving offence. So next Wednesday, having served the visitors' meal and left a cold supper for the family, Lucy joined Chris Stevens in the back of Henry's car.

'We're going to that old inn by the river,' Henry told her. 'They do a very decent meal there and afterwards we can hire a rowing boat.'

Lucy enjoyed the first part of the evening at least more than she had expected. After a couple of glasses of wine Chris lost some of his diffidence, and when they went on the river he turned out to be an extremely competent oarsman, unlike Henry, whose chief talent seemed to be in splashing them! She sat in the stern, trailing one hand in the water, relaxed and well fed, pleasantly idle for once. Fields slid by, then a drinking place for cows. A small wood, and round a bend in the river they came on a low stone wall, broken by a flight of steps. There was a rowing boat tied to an iron ring, and further on a couple leaning on the wall, staring down at the water.

They seemed deep in conversation, heads close together. The man looked a bit like Mark, then he raised his head and it was Mark, waving across at them, with Camilla at his side.

'Hallo there!' he called. 'How far have you come?'

'From the Bell Inn,' answered Henry, gesturing to Chris to pull over. They were under the wall now. Lucy stared straight ahead of her, aware if the others weren't that Camilla had looked anything but pleased to see them.

'You look hot,' smiled Mark, studying Chris's flushed and sweaty face. 'Thirsty work rowing! Care for a drink?'

Henry and Chris were delighted, Caroline neutral. Only Lucy made some attempt to decline. 'It's very kind of you, Mark, but we don't want to intrude——'

'Rubbish!' Mark said briskly, and he descended the stairs and held out a hand to Caroline. Lucy was next, and as his fingers closed on hers to steady her, she felt the familiar agitation that his closeness always brought.

As she reached the top of the steps she came face to face with Camilla. 'Hallo, Dr Fielding,' she said awkwardly. 'I do apologise for—for the intrusion.'

Camilla gave a thin smile and made a conventional reply, then they were walking through the field at the bottom of Mark's garden.

'This is where we shall keep the horses,' said Camilla.

A wicket gate gave on to the garden proper. 'I didn't realise the river was behind that hedge,' Lucy observed, and Camilla asked sharply.

'You've been here before?'

Lucy bit her lip and wished she hadn't spoken. 'We all came one evening. Mark wanted to show us around. You have a lovely place,' she added in an attempt to wipe the frown from the other girl's face.

Surely, surely Camilla wasn't going to make an issue out of a family visit? Just as well she hadn't accepted Mark's invitation to come on her own.

'Have you been down here since the weekend, Miss Fielding?' asked Henry.

Camilla shook her head. 'No, I have a half day, and nothing tomorrow morning until eleven-thirty, so I thought I'd come down again.'

'A long way for such a short visit.'

'But worth it,' Camilla said softly, falling back to join Mark. 'Now that my exams are out of the way I have more time to spare.'

'For which, thank goodness,' Mark murmured, slipping an arm round his fiancée as they strolled over the lawn. 'She did brilliantly, of course, as always.' They exchanged a smile then, two clever, ambitious people who knew where they were going in life, unlike poor Lucy, who felt an acute pang of inferiority in their company. If only she had finished her music studies, she thought forlornly. If only she had some qualifications she wouldn't feel so inadequate.

They went in through the conservatory. 'You look a bit unkempt,' observed Camilla, eyeing Lucy's hair. 'Do you want to tidy yourself? I'll show you the way.'

Caroline, whose hair always stayed in place, didn't come with them. Camilla crossed the wide hall and opened the cloakroom door. It was a relief to get away from the other girl's thinly disguised antagonism. Lucy combed her hair and stared critically at her face. In summertime she always acquired a light dusting of freckles across her nose, though skilful make-up could conceal them, when she bothered to use it. She washed her hands, opened the door and was dismayed to find Camilla still waiting for her.

'By the way, Miss Grant,' Camilla faced her squarely, so that Lucy had to stop, 'I've been thinking of talking to you for quite some time.'

'What about?' asked Lucy, though even before Camilla answered she knew what was coming.

'Please don't think I'm being unkind, my dear'— Camilla's voice was honey sweet—'but you'll only make a fool of yourself if you go on like this.' Lucy stared and said nothing. 'Besides,' Camilla added gently, 'it's so embarrassing for Mark, though he should be used to it by now. So be a good girl and keep out of his way.'

The seconds ticked by. The two girls eyed each other and Lucy's anger mounted. 'Are you suggesting that I'm— I'm trying to take Mark from you?'

'Aren't you?' Camilla's voice was still soft, but now there was an ugly expression on her face. 'Not that you could,' she added contemptuously. 'Mark likes a girl with a bit more to her. You'd bore him in a week, my dear.'

Lucy ignored this cruel remark. 'Has he been complaining about me?' she asked bleakly.

Camilla hesitated, then gave an honest answer. 'No. Mark is so wrapped up in his new job and this house, he doesn't notice what's going on under his nose.'

'Nothing is going on,' Lucy said furiously. 'And if he hasn't noticed, why did you say it was embarrassing for him?'

She felt she had scored a point, but Camilla swept this

away contemptuously. 'He will notice in time, if you persist in forcing yourself on him.'

'Forcing myself? I didn't invite myself to this house that evening. It was entirely Mark's idea. And tonight—to-night it was pure chance.'

'And last Saturday at the fête?'

'Well, for goodness' sake, I always help on a stall.'

'That wasn't what I meant. Mark may not have noticed the way you looked at him, but I did. You're in love with him and you needn't bother to deny it. And if you don't leave him alone I shall tell him so. You wouldn't like that, would you? It would be . . . humiliating, wouldn't it?'

Camilla turned sharply and went back across the hall, and Lucy followed her a few moments later, her cheeks flushed and her heart pounding unpleasantly. Mark was dispensing drinks and there was a good deal of talk and laughter, so that no one seemed to notice her distress. She sat down on the edge of the group and struggled to re-cover her composure, but her thoughts were bitter.

Camilla had said that she was staying for the night. They would be sleeping in that beautiful airy bedroom that Lucy had seen on her last visit. The thought of Camilla and Mark living together, sharing a bed, walking arm in arm through their lovely garden, made Lucy clench her hands in an effort to control her desperate jealousy. Into a gap in the conversation she planted a suggestion that it was time they were on their way.

'No hurry,' Mark said pleasantly, but Camilla had already risen.

'We are a little tired, aren't we, darling? We've been doing a lot of work on the garden.' As they went outside her arm was firmly linked with his, the woman in possession and making it very plain.

'Is she staying there with him?' Caroline asked under her breath, as the rowing boat pulled away from the steps.

Lucy sat with her back to Mark and Camilla, and didn't turn to wave, as Caroline had done. 'I suppose so.' She was carefully casual, though the lump in her throat threatened to choke her.

'On her own?'

'They seemed to be on their own, didn't they?'

'I suppose they sleep together,' Caroline commented sourly. 'Why don't they get married and make it official?'

Henry gave her a reproving look. 'None of our business what they do, is it?'

'Nice Henry,' thought Lucy. At least he was not a spreader of gossip. Caroline went a little pink and fell silent, and Lucy, sitting beside her on the hard wooden seat, struggled to overcome her pain and despair. Camilla had not yet said anything to Mark, but what if she changed her mind? Lucy could picture only too well the amused contempt with which she would throw out some careless remark.

'You know she has a crush on you, darling?' Something like that, or perhaps even more unkind. 'She's made a dead set for you ever since you stayed there, and she's quite unscrupulous about it.'

The question was, would Mark believe her? Tormented by these fantasies, Lucy said very little on the return journey and scarcely noticed when they reached the house that Caroline and Henry stayed in the car, while Chris walked her to the front door.

'Are you doing anything next Saturday?' he asked, giving her his shy but rather charming smile. When she hesitated he added quickly, 'It's my weekend off. I know how you're placed, because Caroline has told me. But you must have some free time. Please, Lucy!'

It was nice to be wanted. It would take her mind off Mark .'I could be free by seven-thirty,' Lucy said slowly. 'I give the visitors an early meal at the weekend, and Susan can wash up.'

'Great!' he exclaimed, leant forward and planted a quick kiss on her cheek. Then he dashed off, calling over his shoulder, 'I'll pick you up then,' and Lucy opened the door, smiling to herself at Chris's behaviour. His diffidence was a refreshing change from the brashness of so many young men. He would not assume that an evening out with a girl should automatically end in lovemaking.

She felt a faint sense of guilt that she had offered him even this amount of encouragement, for she knew he was attracted to her, while on her side there was—what? The beginnings of friendship? Nothing more, certainly, for never in a million years could she feel for the ingenuous Chris what she felt so painfully for Mark.

On Friday evening Chris telephoned and told Lucy sadly that their date was off. His opposite number—had broken his leg hang-gliding. 'So I have to stand in for him, because there's no one else.' He sounded very dejected. 'I'd so looked forward to seeing you, Lucy. I suppose ... no, of course you wouldn't want to ...' His voice tailed off unhappily.

'What were you going to say?' asked Lucy, and he started again, sounding very young and unsure of himself.

'You couldn't bear to come into the hospital for an hour or two, could you?' There was pleading in his voice.

She would only sit and watch television if she stayed at home, for her chief consolation, playing the piano, was seldom available to her these days. One or other of their visitors were nearly always in the sitting-room. It would please Chris if she went and there wasn't that much chance of running into Mark in the evening, even if he was on duty for the weekend.

'All right,' said Lucy. 'I'll come around eight. There's a bus at a quarter to.'

She was made uneasy by the enthusiasm of his reply. She didn't want Chris to fall in love with her. It could only lead to unhappiness for him and embarrassment for her. How complicated human relationships were! How much simpler it would have been if she could have been attracted to Chris instead of to Mark. However, it was Mark she thought about when she lay in bed. Mark with his sharp eyes and his abrupt manner. Mark, who hadn't appeared to notice anything amiss when she and Camilla returned to the drawing-room, but who had held her back for a moment when she was about to climb into the boat.

'You're looking tired, Lucy. Or is it worried? Anything wrong?'

She had smiled and shaken her head, pulled her arm away and jumped into the boat, so that it rocked alarmingly and the others had told her to be careful or she would capsize them.

Camilla had said that Mark was so wrapped up in his own affairs that he didn't notice things. That little incident seemed to prove her wrong.

CHAPTER EIGHT

THE bus station was near the hospital. Lucy went in by the back entrance, that led directly to the residents' quarters, and as she walked across the doctors' car park, she was dismayed to see Mark. He was locking his car, so she walked on quickly, hoping to avoid him.

'Hi, Lucy, what's the rush?'

She stopped reluctantly, because if she went on it would seem peculiar. Mark strode over to her side and smiled down at her. 'What brings you here?'

'Just visiting a—a friend.' She clenched her hands, then put them behind her back. Had Camilla said anything? Would he have come over if she had? Surely not. She relaxed a little and started to walk down the path that led to the residents' house, while Mark accompanied her, chatting amiably about nothing in particular.

It was all right, she thought, with great relief. He didn't know how she felt. Camilla hadn't told him.

Chris had said he would be waiting in the common-room. 'Are you going in here?' asked Mark, stood aside to let her pass and followed her in.

Chris was sprawled on a sofa, reading a newspaper, and he leapt to his feet with a look of delight. 'You've come! I was afraid you'd change your mind.'

'Why should I do that?' Lucy countered, very conscious of Mark only a few feet away, discussing some point with his house surgeon.

While he talked his eyes were on Chris's flushed and eager face.

'Come to my room,' suggested Chris. 'I've got some new Von Karajan recordings that I think you'll like.' It was a bond between them that he was seriously interested in classical music, and Lucy agreed, anxious to get away from Mark.

They played records for two hours, then Chris got a call to the wards and Lucy wandered downstairs to the residents' room, wondering if she might find Caroline there. But her sister, someone told her, was out with Henry.

'They spend most of their free time together,' a woman doctor commented with a knowing smile. This was good news to Lucy, who hoped that something might come of it. She hung on for half an hour or so, not liking to leave without saying goodbye to Chris, and was still waiting for him when Mark came in.

There was no one else in the big room now but Lucy, and his eyebrows went up. 'Still here? You have got it badly!'

'What's that supposed to mean?' she asked crossly.

'Hanging around waiting for the lad. You wouldn't do that if you weren't pretty keen on him, I imagine.'

'Don't be stupid!' she snapped back. 'I like Chris, that's all. I—I felt like a bit of company tonight. You said yourself I should get out more often.'

'So I did,' he agreed, 'but I should have thought you could find someone more exciting than young Chris. I don't suppose he even kissed you while you were up in his room.'

This was true, and Lucy had been relieved that he hadn't. Now, subjected to Mark's teasing, she almost wished that she could deny it. She was still trying to think of a suitably snubbing reply when Chris returned, full of apologies for his long absence.

'Couldn't you stay on a bit?' he asked. But when Lucy said that the last bus left in ten minutes he accepted it gracefully, and walked with her to the hospital exit. He stood there for a second, looking at her, then he put his hands on her shoulders and planted a quick clumsy kiss on her mouth.

'Goodnight, Lucy. Thanks a lot for coming.' As he

rushed off Mark's car came slowly down the drive. She walked on quickly, hoping he hadn't seen that brief embrace. It really was rotten luck, thought Lucy, that she had kept bumping into him tonight.

There was a light toot behind her and she swung round as Mark drew in to the edge of the pavement. 'Very touching,' he commented with a grin. 'It would seem to disprove what you said a few minutes ago.'

'Oh, go away!' she muttered, and laughing, he rolled up his window and drove on.

She wondered why he felt this urge to get at her. He had always been inclined to tease, perhaps because she responded so readily. However, if he believed she was interested in Chris it might be a good thing. If Camilla was malicious enough to carry out her threat, he would probably dismiss it as the figment of a jealous imagination.

On Monday morning Caroline telephoned. 'Sorry I missed you the other night. Henry took me to a play in Birmingham.' She went on to explain that the hospital secretary had asked her to find out if Lucy had any rooms free. 'There's a locum senior registrar coming next week, an Australian chap. He wanted a hospital apartment, but there isn't one available, so Mr. Williams thought our place might do.'

'I'm flattered,' said Lucy.

'You should be. There are plenty of other places, but Mark told him how comfortable he'd been, and the two rooms are almost like an apartment.'

'And you wouldn't mind?'

'Mind? Why should I mind?' asked Caroline, for all the world as if she had never raised the most violent objections to her sister running a boarding house.

Lucy smiled to herself and said that the rooms would be free today week. Should she ring the secretary and tell him?

'Do that,' said Caroline. 'Oh, and Lucy, you were right about Henry. He is nice!' She said this almost shyly, gave a funny little half laugh and added a quick goodbye.

Lucy stood by the telephone for a minute or two, thinking about Caroline. It sounded as if she was over Mark completely, and well on the way to falling in love with nice Henry Wilson. How ironic that she, who had urged her sister to be sensible, should find it so hard to be sensible herself.

'Morning, Miss Grant. Can you tell me where to find the nearest newsagent?' That was one of the visitors, poking his head round the dining-room door, a Westhampton businessman who hadn't seemed to grasp the fact that the country didn't offer the same amenities as a city.

'The village shop stocks them, but only on order. I'm afraid you'll have to go into Barnslow.'

'I can't waste the time,' he said crossly. 'I have to be in Cardiff before eleven.'

'It isn't far into Barnslow,' murmured Lucy, but as she sorted through the laundry in the washroom, she wondered if their house might be unsuitable for a registrar. Consultants had fewer emergency calls than their juniors. It had suited Mark, but the Australian might want to be closer to the hospital.

'I don't think that will matter, Miss Grant,' said the secretary, when Lucy raised this point later on the telephone. 'He's medical, not surgical, and they're not called out quite so often, are they?'

It was decided that Dr Cassidy should come out to see her next Monday, to decide if he liked the place. 'I wouldn't dare book it without his approval,' Mr Williams said with a sigh. 'These overseas doctors can be very fussy, you know. I'm tired of hearing how run-down our hospitals in Britain are, and what appalling facilities we offer our residents.'

Lucy laughed. 'Well, Barnslow General is pretty decrepit, but Caroline says it does jolly good work, and that's what counts, isn't it?'

They parted amicably and Lucy thought happily that

she might well have a regular clientele from the hospital, for locums came and went not only in the holiday season, but even in the winter months when people were taking study leave.

Dr Cassidy arrived bright and early the following Monday morning, for a quick look-see, as he put it, then stayed for quite a long time, chatting to Lucy over a cup of coffee. He was tanned, athletic-looking and extremely likeable. She was pleased that he approved so wholeheartedly of the rooms.

'They're great, Miss Grant. We don't have places like this in Australia,' and he glanced admiringly round the old farmhouse kitchen.

He moved in that evening and by next day he was on christian name terms with the whole family, except for Mr Grant. Susan fell for him on sight, laughed at his Australian accent and was teased in return for her snooty Pommie voice.

'I had no idea there were so many glamorous doctors around,' she mused, when they were alone in the kitchen one evening. 'Do you think I'd make a good nurse, Lucy?'

'Terrible,' smiled Lucy. 'You wouldn't like having to put your hair up.'

'And for every glamorous doctor there are probably a hundred short fat ones,' added William with a grin.

Susan ignored this, continuing with her own line of thought. 'He's even nicer than Mark, don't you agree?'

'No, I don't,' William said bluntly.

'So friendly and informal. Mark took longer to unbend.'

'Good thing too,' grunted her brother. 'I don't like people who are too chummy when they hardly know you.' William was reserved by nature, preferring to assess a person thoroughly before he gave his approval.

'Well, I think he's beaut,' said Susan, airily appropriating a piece of Australian slang, and William looked disgusted.

'Do you have to be so corny? Last week it was phoney

American,' for these days the Grants' visitors covered a wide range of nationalities.

Running a boarding house had turned out to be fun, even though it was extremely hard work. Falling into bed each night, tired but fulfilled, Lucy often told herself that she had made the right choice. The family would have hated moving into a small house in Barnslow, and they had all come to accept the presence of strangers in their midst, even her father, though he was reluctant to admit it. He had smartened himself up lately, perhaps due to the influence of his psychiatrist, whom he was seeing weekly at the hospital.

Life was treating the Grant family more kindly in every way, thought Lucy, determined to be cheerful even though her own problems were unresolved. How did you get over a man when you thought about him all the time? How did you stop yourself thinking about him? Mark had been in his new house over a month by now. Was he happy there? Too busy to be lonely? Was he any good at cooking or did he eat most of his meals out? However often she told herself that it was nothing to do with her, these thoughts would float into her mind at the most inopportune moments.

One day, in the middle of a game of tennis, she found herself indulging in a foolish daydream, imagining that it was Mark who was partnering her on the hospital courts, and not Kevin Cassidy.

'Concentrate, girl!' yelled Kevin as an easy ball sailed past Lucy.

She gave a guilty smile and admitted that her thoughts had been wandering.

'You'll never improve if you don't concentrate,' Kevin admonished her. 'It's the key to the game. You like to win, don't you?'

'I don't really mind,' said Lucy, and he rolled his eyes disgustedly.

'How typically British! Aussies like to win.'

'Then you'd better pick another partner,' for Kevin and she had played together on several occasions.

He put a hand on her shoulder and his teeth gleamed in his deeply tanned face. 'I don't want another partner. I want you.'

The August sun was very hot, and Lucy blinked in its glare, not sure if his words held a double meaning. He moved his hand down her bare arm, his blue eyes intent and questioning.

'Break it up, you two!' shouted the young doctor who was playing against them, and his partner, a staff nurse, added caustically, 'There's a queue for the court, so while you're on it stick to tennis!'

Lucy coloured, but Kevin only laughed. The staff nurse was a thin girl with a sharp manner, and Lucy had an idea that she would have welcomed a change of partners. Kevin was already very popular at the hospital, a tribute to his cheerful, extrovert personality. The staff nurse had looked Lucy up and down when they met before the game, and had reminded Kevin that outsiders weren't supposed to use the hospital courts. There was such a run on them that it wasn't really fair.

'Jealous because your legs are better than hers, honey.' Kevin had commented, as he and Lucy walked to their side of the net. He was always making remarks like that. He probably did to all the girls, Lucy reminded herself, though it was flattering to be admired. Flattering to have two men showing an interest in her, for Chris was more attentive than ever, and showed open disapproval of her friendship with Kevin.

'You shouldn't encourage him, Lucy. He's been out with half the girls in the hospital and he's only been here three weeks.'

'Then you must be very understaffed,' Lucy had joked, and he had scowled at her, his nice boyish face flushed and angry.

'You know what I mean. The fellow's a real womaniser.

I don't like him living in your house.'

By the standards of many young doctors Chris was inclined to be prim. He was probably exaggerating about Kevin and Lucy paid very little attention to his remarks.

They lost the set, then had to stop because another quartet were waiting for the court.

'Pity,' said Kevin. 'Could we hire a court in town next time, and play a proper match?'

They were relaxing on the grass, discussing this and watching the next players warming up, when a troop of white-coated doctors approached. It was Mark, walking at his usual brisk pace, flanked by his registrar and two housemen. He slowed down when he saw Lucy, and stopped beside them, his eyes travelling over her flushed face and dishevelled hair.

'You look hot, Lucy. I didn't know you played.'

'I'm not very good,' she confessed. 'We were easily beaten.'

Kevin rolled over and ran a finger down one of her slim brown legs. 'When a girl looks as good as she does in shorts, it doesn't matter so much what her game is like!'

Mark's lips tightened and the look he gave Kevin was disapproving in the extreme. 'I should concentrate on the game, Cassidy, then you'd be more likely to win.'

'Snooty bastard,' Kevin commented, making no effort to lower his voice, though Mark had moved on so quickly he might well have been out of earshot. 'Do you know him well, Lucy?'

She told him how she had got to know Mark, and Kevin gave his broad grin. 'Bet he wasn't as easy as I am. Admit it, girl—I'm your favourite lodger!'

The staff nurse, looking irritated by Kevin's banter, said she was on duty after tea. The other young doctor jumped up and Kevin offered Lucy a hand, continuing to hold hers as they strolled back towards the doctors' quarters. He was still holding it when they met Mark and his colleagues, returning from the pathology block. Selfconscious, Lucy looked anywhere but at Mark, and gave furtive little tugs in an effort to free herself. Kevin's grip tightened and he swung his racket nonchalantly. Hot-cheeked, she passed within a foot or two of Mark, for the path was a narrow one and she couldn't avoid going close to him.

She kept her eyes down, but even so she sensed his disapproval. Kevin's brand of humour would not appeal to Mark's more fastidious nature. He would never embarrass a girl publicly in the way that the Australian had done.

A few evenings later, when Lucy was washing the dishes and William was tinkering with a transistor radio at the kitchen table, there was a knock on the back door and Mark walked in. He greeted them both pleasantly, and said he had been meaning to look in for quite a time. He talked first about how he was getting on in his new house.

'I'm living out of tins,' he admitted, when Lucy asked how he was coping with the cooking. 'Perhaps you could give me some simple recipes, Lucy?'

She had returned to the kitchen sink after a carefully polite greeting. She wished she could show William's uninhibited enthusiasm for Mark's arrival. She might have done if she had not been in love with him.

'I'll lend you a cookery book,' she said, without turning round.

Mark sat down beside William and examined his book on transistor circuits. 'Don't you find it rather tough?' he asked, but William shook his head.

'I find it quite easy. Physics is my best subject.'

Mark looked impressed. 'Is it indeed! You're a very bright boy, then.' He rose again and crossed the room, stood behind Lucy and undid her apron strings. 'You've finished the dishes,' he said impatiently. 'Stop messing about.'

She turned round, her heart beating more rapidly. There was something about Mark's manner that made her wary. She couldn't have defined what it was, but she sensed that this was more than a social visit.

'Would you like coffee, Mark?' she asked.

He shook his head. 'Later, maybe. Walk round the garden with me.'

'I'd rather sit down. I'm—I'm a little tired.'

'Then we'll sit on the bench.' He took her by the arm and walked her towards the door. She didn't want an argument in front of William, so she allowed herself to be led into the garden. Mark walked briskly towards the shrubbery, ignoring the seat near the front of the house. When they were screened from anyone looking out of the windows, he swung round to face her.

'How long is Cassidy staying with you?' he asked abruptly. At her look of surprise he asked again, 'How long, Lucy?'

'I've no idea. Several weeks, I suppose. A couple of months, maybe. Why do you ask?'

Mark frowned and dug his heel into the ground. 'I find this hard to say——'

'Then don't,' she cut in, guessing what was to come.

'But Cassidy has a bad reputation where women are concerned. Already, after such a short time in Barnslow.'

'Really, Mark?' she said coolly. 'I'm rather ... surprised that you feel you have to tell me.'

He shoved his hands in his pockets, walked up and down a couple of times and came back to her. 'You think I'm interfering—that it's none of my business—but I'm very fond of you all. You're the first friends I made when I came here.'

Touched by this remark, Lucy conceded that he was acting out of genuine interest in her welfare. 'But honestly, Mark, it's quite unnecessary. I know what Kevin's like, and I don't take him seriously.'

'Keep it that way, then. Don't encourage him.' His eyes travelled down her slim but shapely figure, and rested on her legs for a moment. 'Do you have to wear those things?' he asked irritably.

It had been a blistering hot day, the sort of day on which Lucy would have loved to swim. Since she couldn't spare the time, she had put on the briefest clothes she had, navy denim shorts and a skimpy white top. She leant against a tree trunk and swung one of her sandals on her bare toes.

'You're not suggesting I dress like this for Kevin's benefit?'

'You know he admires you in shorts.'

She stared, at a loss for a moment, then she remembered Kevin's remarks on the tennis court. The surprising thing was that Mark had. A little colour came into her cheeks and she told him crossly that she dressed to please herself. 'I had an hour free this afternoon, so I put on my bikini. I suppose you think that was being provocative?'

Unexpectedly Mark laughed. 'Depends where you lay. And who was around.'

She laughed too. 'Everyone was out. I'm not a complete idiot, Mark. I know what some of the male visitors are like.'

He frowned. 'Have you had trouble with any of them?'

'None I couldn't handle,' Lucy said quietly.

'You're too young to be running this place,' he said abruptly, 'And your father's no help at all.'

Back in the kitchen he declined a coffee, saying it was too hot. 'Are you two alone? How about coming over to my place for a swim?'

William jumped up, but Lucy looked at Mark doubtfully. 'How would we get back? There may not be a bus. And I'm expecting a call soon from Dad. He and Susan are staying with our aunt and uncle in Devon.'

He said impatiently that her father could ring again. And of course he would bring them back. 'So get your bathing things, William.'

'Yes, you go, William,' said Lucy. 'I've a lot to do this evening.'

'You must have some time off,' Mark said firmly, but still she hesitated.

'Will anyone else be there?' she asked. By anyone she meant Camilla, of course.

Mark's mouth quirked. 'Just us. Come on, Lucy.'

So she went, not too reluctantly, because the thought of a swim was very attractive, and probably Camilla would never know. Mark apologised for the pool, which was cracked in places, but said the builders hadn't had time to repair it yet. However, the water was clean and deliciously cool, and the three of them played around until it was nearly dark. When they finally left the pool Mark showed Lucy to a bedroom, where she could change, and by the time she came down again the other two were relaxing in the drawing-room. Mark had a short drink in his hand, and William a tall glass that clinked with ice. They were absorbed in a conversation about nuclear power, for William took a keen interest in the energy crisis and knew more about it than many adults.

Lucy slid into a seat and listened to them. Mark poured her a drink and the talk shifted to his affairs. The house was coming on well, but he was behind with the garden and he wanted to get it tidied up before winter.

William offered to help him. 'I've lots of spare time in the holidays. I could bike over most days.'

'Aren't you going away?' asked Mark.

'Susan and Dad have gone to Aunt Mary's, but I'd rather stay here.' Aunt Mary treated William as if he was still a little boy, so he had dug his heels in and refused to go this year. Lucy would have liked him to have a proper holiday, but they couldn't afford it.

Mark looked thoughtful, then agreed that it would be helpful to have William do some gardening. 'But on the strict understanding that I pay you something.' William went red and mumbled something about not suggesting it if he'd thought Mark would say that, but Mark cut him short. 'I know, old chap, but I insist. Why shouldn't you earn some pocket money? And you can combine work with pleasure. Use the pool any time you like.'

It was gone eleven when they returned home. As they drove into the courtyard the lights on another car dimmed, and Kevin Cassidy strolled out of the barn. He squinted into the headlights, then stood waiting for Lucy to get out.

Mark drove off immediately and William went ahead of them into the house.

'Wasn't that Franklin's car?' asked Kevin.

'That's right.'

'See much of him these days?'

'Now and then.' They went into the kitchen, which was empty. 'We were swimming in his pool,' Lucy added.

'You do know he's engaged?'

'Of course I know,' she said irritably, then the absurdity of it struck her and she started to laugh. When she could speak again she explained her mirth. 'It's the absolute end! Mark warns me about you, and you think I shouldn't go out with an engaged man. I wouldn't have expected you to be so stuffy.'

'Only thinking of your welfare, honey.' He slid off the table and put his hands on her shoulders. 'Franklin's fiancée sends shivers down my spine. She could turn real nasty if she thought you were poaching on her preserves.'

Lucy wriggled out from under his hands. Kevin was inclined to touch her at every opportunity; it was something about him for which she didn't much care. 'I know what Camilla's like,' she said quietly. 'And swimming in his pool hardly ranks as poaching, especially with William there. I'm tired, Kevin. I'm going to bed.'

'Just a moment. What did Franklin say about me?'

'He warned me you were a bit of a wolf.' From the safety of the door Lucy smiled back at him. 'And I'll tell you something, Kevin. I think he was right!'

William was a reliable boy; if he said he would do something he did it. Nearly every day he bicycled over to Mark's place, often with a packed lunch, always with his swimming trunks in his saddlebag. Lucy wasn't entirely happy about the arrangement, though it did give her brother something definite to do. August being the main holiday month, most of his friends were away, so he might have found time heavy on his hands if he hadn't been going to Mark's. Her worry was on Camilla's account. Would the girl extend her dislike of Lucy to Lucy's brother? She probed a little, but William was maddeningly vague. He had only seen Camilla a couple of times. She was hardly ever down. He passed on an invitation of Mark's to come over for the day tomorrow, swim, have a game of tennis.

'We've rolled the court, Luce, and Mark's bought a net.'

'You know I can't spare a whole day,' protested Lucy.

'Yes, you can. You said we were going to have a week-end to ourselves for once.'

Lucy had made this decision at the beginning of the week, feeling that she had earned a couple of days off. Kevin had said he would be going away, and her father and Susan were still down at her aunt's place. It was an ideal time for a short break. She was tempted, but felt it would be unwise to accept. The less she saw of Mark the better.

'A weekend without visitors will give me a chance to catch up on the chores,' she said firmly.

So next morning, soon after breakfast, William cycled off on his own. 'When are you leaving, Kevin?' Lucy asked, as she cleared the dishes from the dining-room.

Kevin had come down late and shuddered when she offered him bacon and eggs. He had eaten nothing and was on his third cup of black coffee. 'When I've resuscitated myself, honey. We had quite a party last night.' He slouched in his chair with easy grace, a very attractive man, whom it was impossible not to like, even if she didn't quite approve of him.

He had said something about going up to London. 'Will you be back tomorrow night?' Lucy asked, and he nodded.

'Worse luck! I'd have liked a job in the sinful city, but Barnslow was the best I could find.'

She explained that he was the only visitor. 'So I might take Sunday off. I'll leave the key in the garage in case you're back before me.'

Kevin looked thoughtful. 'You mean you're on your own? Then come to London with me.'

When she said that William would be back that evening he dismissed this with a flick of his fingers. 'The boy's old enough to stay on his own for one night. Do come, Lucy.'

It was years since she had been to London, and if the invitation had been just for the day she might have accepted. But she was not, as she had told Mark, a complete fool. A weekend with Kevin would have been asking for trouble. So she declined with a smile, and he grinned as if he knew very well what was in her mind.

'O.K., honey,' he said equably. 'Then how about a run down to the coast today?' He looked out of the wide open window at the sun-drenched garden. 'London would be hellishly hot at that. Know any good beaches in Wales?'

The chores had only been an excuse not to accept Mark's invitation, and she hadn't been to the seaside since last summer. Kevin could be very persuasive, so an hour later Lucy stood at the gate, waiting for Kevin's car to roll out of the yard. As she shut the gate behind him she heard the distant sound of the telephone in the house. 'I won't be a minute,' she called, opening the gate again.

'Leave it,' shouted Kevin, 'If it's important they'll ring back,' so she climbed in beside him and they set off for Barnslow, where they would join the main road to the Welsh coast. Lucy was taking him to her favourite beach, which had got more crowded over the years, but was large enough to accommodate many hundreds of people.

The tide was far out when they arrived, so they walked nearly two miles along the sands to the end where few people bothered to go. They walked at the edge of the water and Lucy splashed through the shallow surf, her canvas shoes in her hand, while Kevin strode along on the still wet sand.

'You're like a little kid on the first day of the holidays,' he remarked, and Lucy, smiling back at him, said that it had been a great idea. She only wished they were stopping for longer.

'Then why don't we? Bound to be somewhere we could find for the night.' He said it casually, but his sideways squint held a hint of calculation.

'I told you, Kevin, I don't want to leave William on his own.'

'You mollycoddle that boy, but if you won't leave him why don't you ring up Franklin and ask him to keep William for the night?'

Lucy smiled to herself at this idea. Mark would say some pretty trenchant things if she told him why she was asking such a favour! Not that it was any of his business where she chose to stay, or with whom. She found his habit of interfering in her affairs excessively irritating and rather puzzling. She supposed he treated her as a sort of younger sister or cousin, and an immature one at that. If only, just once, he would see her as a woman! If only, Lucy thought regretfully, she was down here with Mark instead of with Kevin. It was such a perfect day, the August heat tempered by a brisk little breeze that blew off the sea, creaming the small waves at her feet. She would show Mark the small cove round the headland, which was nearly always empty, because it involved a scramble over sharply tilted rocks. They would talk about everything under the sun, his work, his house, music, gardening ... Then Kevin said something and Lucy snapped out of her daydream, feeling very guilty because she was being ungrateful.

It was Kevin who had brought her down, and she owed it to him to be a good companion. So she splashed over to his side, determinedly bright, and he slid an arm around her as they walked along. He kept it there as he dumped the rucksack on the sand, at the spot he had selected for their picnic. It was a cleft in the rocks running back twenty feet or so, only visible to people standing right opposite the entrance. When he kissed her Lucy stood passively, her arms by her side. She was not going to encourage him by an ardent response; she didn't want her lovely day spoilt by quarrels over lovemaking.

Kevin was not insensitive. He let her go, smiling faintly. 'Plenty of time,' he murmured. 'Shall we swim?'

When they came back from the sea Lucy spread her towel just outside the cleft, which lay now in shadow. 'Warmer here,' she observed, and Kevin, with a goodhumoured shrug, joined her.

She rubbed suntan lotion on to her arms and the front of her body, then Kevin took the bottle from her and slapped some on her back. His hands moved over her, warm, caressing, intimate. 'That's enough,' Lucy said quickly, her breath coming faster than usual. She moved away from him, on to the hot sand.

Kevin's eyes glinted. 'So you do have normal reactions! I was beginning to wonder!'

He covered the gap between them and pushed her down, so that they lay close together, his hand behind her head to prevent her from drawing away. When he kissed her this time she responded, her inhibitions released by sun and sea and physical contact with an attractive and experienced man. His other hand moved over her body and his kisses became more insistent. He raised his head for a moment to glance along the beach. There were only a few people about, but Lucy was glad of their presence. She might have found Kevin difficult to handle if they had been quite alone.

As it was she felt suddenly self-conscious. 'Kevin ... please!' She pushed him away and scrambled to her feet. 'It's a—a little public for that sort of thing,' and turning she ran down to the sea again.

'Come back!' Kevin shouted. 'I want my lunch,' but she

stayed away for ten minutes or so, taking a quick dip, then lying at the edge of the water and wondering if she had made a mistake in coming here with the Australian. Some men could be very persistent, and she didn't want to spend the day fighting off Kevin's embraces. It might be better to have it out with him now.

Slowly she walked back up the beach, to find that he had opened a can of beer and was investigating what she had packed for lunch. 'Kevin, I'm sorry if I'm here under false pretences.'

'In what way, honey?' He took a ham roll and bit into it.

'I mean, you may have thought—coming out for the day with you—that I didn't mind——' She was finding it hard to say.

Kevin, mouth full of ham roll, surveyed her sardonically. Colouring under his worldly, knowing gaze, Lucy struggled on. 'I'm not the sort of girl who goes in for casual love-making. I suppose you'll wish now that you hadn't brought me?'

Kevin swallowed and continued to stare at her. 'It's a free world, little girl. Perhaps you'll change your mind!' Or I'll change it for you, that look seemed to say. 'If you don't hurry up and have something to eat, there'll be nothing left,' he added, reaching for a second roll.

'I brought plenty,' said Lucy, feeling more relaxed now that she had got things straight.

They stayed on the beach until the tide had rolled back in, although they had to leave their picnic spot by four o'clock, for fear of being cut off.

'Though I'd have been quite happy to spend a few hours up there!' Kevin gestured with a grin towards a wide, grassy ledge twenty feet above them, and overhung by a rocky outcrop, that would hide it from anyone above.

Lucy ignored this remark and finished packing the haver-sack. They had had a good time together. They were both strong swimmers and they had had a lot of fun. Kevin talked of bringing her down again and hiring a boat maybe.

He was an experienced sailor, having grown up in a family who owned a sailing dinghy. They could make enquiries on their way back through the village.

They stopped for a meal at a delightful old pub in mid-Wales. Kevin was attentive and amusing and not in the least amorous. He drank sparingly, but filled Lucy's glass up several times with the mellow wine he had chosen for them.

'I believe you're trying to make me sozzled,' said Lucy, only half jokingly, and his teeth gleamed in an answering smile.

'You don't have much opinion of me, do you, honey? My approach is a little more subtle than that.'

He had a way of looking at her that made Lucy's heart beat faster. Could you be attracted to a man of whom you didn't really approve? Of course you could, and she was. It was a superficial thing and bore no resemblance to what she felt for Mark. If Mark had kissed her as Kevin had done, she would not have been able to draw back so easily. She gave a small unconscious sigh, and Kevin leant forward to put his hand over hers.

'Sometimes I have the feeling you're only half with me. What is it, Lucy? What were you thinking about?'

She coloured and withdrew her hand. 'I'm sorry, Kevin. My thoughts were wandering for a moment.'

'They often do,' he said drily. 'It's a man, isn't it? Anyone I know?'

Faced with this direct question, Lucy blushed and stammered and looked helplessly around. They were cut off in a small recess, just the two of them with no one within earshot. Kevin took pity on her.

'Keep your cool, sweetie. And your secret if you want to,' he added carelessly, a man who believed in skating through life without getting too deeply involved, on a personal level at any rate. His work he took very seriously.

CHAPTER NINE

THEY arrived back at ten-thirty to find William waiting for them in the kitchen. 'Where have you been?' he demanded crossly. 'You said you had a lot to do.'

'I changed my mind,' Lucy retorted gaily, buoyed up by good food and wine. 'Kevin and I went to Castle Bay. It was absolutely great.'

This was one of William's favourite places too, but he stared at her unsmilingly. 'Big deal,' he muttered. 'Mark was disappointed that you didn't come.'

Kevin had lowered himself into a chair and stuck his feet out in front of him. He sat up at William's remark and looked very hard at Lucy. 'You didn't break a date to come out with me?' he enquired.

Lucy shook her head, annoyed with William for being difficult. 'Of course I didn't. Mark said something about us both going to his place, but——'

'But a day with me was more attractive,' Kevin interposed.

'Bighead,' William muttered under his breath.

Lucy could have banged their heads together. 'But I'd already made up my mind to stay at home,' she added, and saw her mistake too late.

'Until I changed your mind for you,' said Kevin smugly. 'I'm flattered, honey, that I rate higher than Franklin does!'

'Oh, don't be so silly!' snapped Lucy, and then, remembering what a good time he had given her, 'I'm sorry, Kevin, but can't we drop it?'

He was not easily offended. 'Of course,' he agreed. 'Isn't it time for your bed, Billy boy?'

'Only Susan calls me Billy,' her brother replied in a

dignified manner that had the odd effect of making him seem younger than his fourteen years. He gave Kevin a look of dislike. 'Why don't *you* go to bed? I want to talk to my sister.'

'William! That was very rude.' Lucy bit back an urge to laugh, because the look on Kevin's face was so comical.

On the drive back from the inn he had been casually amorous, in words if not in action—telling her what a little beaut she was, that she had the prettiest legs he had ever seen, that her skin was smooth as silk. Platitudes which he probably used on all his girl-friends. When Lucy had said this he denied it indignantly.

'If I can't say something nice about a girl I keep quiet. You must know you're very pretty,' and he had added meaningfully, 'I hope that young brother of yours isn't around when we get back.'

Disappointed in this, he rose abruptly. 'I think I'll skip that drink, Lucy.' The look he gave William was uncharitable in the extreme.

'Good riddance,' muttered William as the door closed behind the Australian. 'What do you see in him, Luce? And how could you possibly prefer going out with him to a day at Mark's place?'

'It was so hot today,' Lucy said placatingly, 'and a day by the sea seemed just the thing.'

'Mark would have taken you if you'd asked him. He rang you when I arrived without you, and then quite a few times during the day. He was absolutely determined that you shouldn't stay on your own, slogging away at housework.'

'That was kind of him,' Lucy said briskly. 'Shall we drop it now, William? There's no need to go on and on.'

Next morning William said he was going to Mark's place again. Lucy, a little uneasy at being left alone all day with Kevin, decided to pick plums from the small orchard at the bottom of the garden. She laid breakfast for one in the dining-room, propped a note up against the cereal packet and went outside. There was no need to stand on ceremony with Kevin; he was quite prepared to fend for himself if he came down late.

An hour later he appeared at the foot of the plum tree and smiled up at her. 'Come on down, Lucy. The day is ours.'

She shook her head. 'I've work to do, Kevin. Yesterday was great, but I can't take another one off.'

When he realised that she wasn't to be persuaded he shrugged rather irritably and left her, throwing a remark over his shoulder that she only half caught. She thought he said that he would be gone all day, something about seeing who was around at the hospital. Doubtless there would be more than one nurse who would jump at the chance of a day out in the medical registrar's company. He was popular and generous with his money. He knew how to give a girl a good time, and if he expected more in return than some girls were prepared to give, that was a common enough masculine attitude these days.

Lucy finished filling her basket with the bright red fruit, pulled it out of the fork in the tree trunk where she had wedged it, and swung herself to the ground. She had climbed all the trees in the orchard during her childhood, and knew every foot and hand-hold. She tipped the contents carefully into her wheelbarrow and was preparing to climb up again when she heard a car turn into the yard.

Kevin come back for something? But he had left quite a time ago. She was about to investigate when Mark's tall figure came round the side of the house, striding purposefully towards her. For one joyful moment she thought he had come to take her back with him. She would have gone willingly today, she was so pleased to see him. Then he was close enough to read his expression and she knew that he was not here to issue an invitation.

His mouth was compressed, his eyes narrowed, and he

held himself stiffly in the way he did when he was annoyed about something.

Lucy stood by the tree and waited for him to speak, while Beryl ambled up to him, tail wagging enthusiastically. Mark bent to pat the old dog, then straightened and gave her an unsmiling look.

'I'd begun to think you'd gone out again with Cassidy. Is he around?'

'No, he isn't. He went off for the day.'

'Without you?' he snapped. 'I am surprised.'

'As a matter of fact,' said Lucy, determinedly casual, though her own temper was beginning to rise, 'he did ask me out, but I had a lot to do.'

Mark gave a contemptuous snort. 'Is that your permanent excuse when you want to turn down an invitation? What's your game, Lucy? Playing hard to get? It won't work with a man like Cassidy.'

'I'm not playing any game,' Lucy retorted, hanging on to her self control with a great effort. It would be undignified to start wrangling with Mark, and besides, he had a knack of winning most of their arguments. She reached above her head, caught hold of a branch and swung herself back into the tree.

'I haven't finished talking to you,' Mark said grimly, and a hard grip closed around her ankle.

'Let me go!' Lucy muttered between her teeth.

'I'll pull if I have to.'

'All right! All right!' Furious, she jumped down to face him, flushed with anger. 'I don't know what this is all about, Mark, but you're being extremely offensive. And interfering,' she added, her voice beginning to rise.

'Someone has to interfere,' he said quietly. 'I told you the other day what Cassidy is like.'

'That's your opinion! Which I didn't ask you for anyway.'

'I know that, but I can't stand by and see you get hurt. Cassidy is a type I've often met in hospital—drifting from country to country, a year in the States, a year in England, picking up women in each new place, then passing on to other conquests. He boasts about it too.' Mark's face registered distaste. 'Do you want to be talked about in that sort of way?'

She hesitated, knowing in her heart that he was speaking the truth.

'Well?' he asked sharply, put his hands on her shoulders and gave her an impatient shake.

'Let me go!' she exclaimed. 'Don't do that, Mark! I'm not a child, though you treat me like one. I'm quite capable of managing my own affairs.'

'Are you?' he asked softly. 'William said you'd had too much to drink last night.'

Lucy registered a very black mark against her young brother. 'What absolute nonsense!'

He ignored this. 'A well-known softening-up technique,' he added nastily. 'Or had he already had what he wanted?'

Outraged, she swung her hand up to hit his face, but he caught it in mid-air. 'Well? Has he made love to you?' he ground out.

She tugged unavailingly. 'It's none of your business!'

'*Has he?*'

'What do you think?' Lucy asked mockingly. 'We found a nice secluded spot on the beach.' She smiled at the remembrance of Kevin's arms around her. 'We had ... a lot of fun!' It seemed that the words were coming out of their own volition, that she had no control over them. She wanted to shock him, for reasons that weren't at all clear to her. 'We were disappointed to find William around when we got back,' she added, and gave him an impudent smile.

He let her go abruptly and the contempt on his face seared her to the heart. 'God, what a fool I've been!' he said savagely, 'thinking you were a little innocent who needed protection. While all the time—all the time——' He ran out of words, raked his hands through his hair, then turned away without looking at her again. He walked slowly along the path to the wicket gate, stopped and turned to stare at her.

'William's only fourteen,' he said heavily. 'It's an age for ideals. I shouldn't like him to see Cassidy coming out of your bedroom.' He opened the gate and went through it.

Lucy stood open-mouthed, horrified by the effect of her words. Why, why had she been so foolish? Hinted at an affair, where none existed? She was just about to run after him when she heard his car start up and knew it was too late.

Heavily, wearily, she climbed back into the plum tree and went on picking. Her eyes filled with tears, so that she could scarcely see what she was doing. She wiped them away with the back of her other hand, but they came again, pouring down her cheeks. Would Mark believe her now, if she told him Kevin had done no more than kiss her? Why had she wanted him to believe otherwise? She reached out to her fullest extent, her father's old walking stick in her hand, attempting to hook a high branch down, but misjudged the distance, because her vision was blurred by tears, stretched too far and overbalanced.

She crashed down through the lower branches and struck the ground heavily, one leg twisted under her. Half stunned, winded, she lay on her side, then beginning to recover, she tried to sit up, but the searing pain in her thigh made her cry out and she collapsed again, sick and fainting. The sky seemed to have darkened and there was a curious roaring sound in her ears. Waves of nausea engulfed her, and she lay helplessly, while Beryl sniffed agitatedly at her, ran backwards and forwards several times and ended by settling beside her. The old dog licked her face, loving and uneasy.

'Oh, Beryl,' Lucy whispered, 'if only someone would come!'

Mercifully William was not spending all day at Mark's. He arrived back at one o'clock and yelled for his sister. 'Lucy! Luce-ee! Where are you?'

She called weakly, then tried to persuade Beryl to go to him, but Beryl refused to budge. In the end he found her, his rosy cheeks paling, so that the freckles stood out against the white skin.

'Are you badly hurt, Lucy? Can't you get up?'

She shook her head. 'It's ... my leg ... I think I've broken it ... and there's an awful pain in my stomach ...'

'Oh, g-gosh,' he stammered. 'What shall I d-do?'

'Call the doctor,' Lucy managed. 'No, call an ambulance. It would be quicker—I'll have to go to hospital anyway. And then you'd better let Caro know, if she's free.'

Her brother shot off and was back surprisingly quickly, a cushion in his hand. He raised her head gently and slid the cushion under it, then sat beside her on the grass and held her hand.

'I rang Mark,' he said quietly. 'He's more use than Caro, and it would only worry her if she wasn't free. He's coming at once. He said if the ambulance arrives first not to wait for him, he'll meet us in the Accident Department.'

However, Mark beat the ambulance, came running into the orchard, knelt and examined her quickly and competently. As his gentle hands moved over her body, Lucy knew that she had to remember something—something Mark had said to her, something unpleasant. Only she couldn't concentrate. She felt lightheaded, as if she was about to float away. She sensed that Mark was very worried about her condition, though his expression was carefully controlled, tried to ask him how badly she was hurt, but couldn't get the words out.

Half conscious, she was hardly aware of the ambulance men splinting her right leg a few minutes later, of them lifting her carefully on to a stretcher, of the drive to the Accident Department.

She came round in a small white-walled room with swing doors, that seemed to open and close continually. Men in white coats came and went, nurses did things to her, someone asked her when she had last eaten, someone else gave her an injection.

'What's happening?' she croaked. 'Where's Mark?'

'I'm here, little one.' He materialised like a genie, a middle-aged man with a round cheerful face by his side. 'You've ruptured your spleen and you'll have to have an operation.'

She stared at her arm, which was connected to a piece of tubing. 'What's that?' she asked.

'A blood transfusion. Caroline will be coming just as soon as she's finished assisting in Theatre.'

'Are you going to operate?'

'No,' he said calmly, 'I never operate on my friends. Dr Berrington will be looking after you,' and he indicated the man by his side, who smiled reassuringly at Lucy and told her they would be meeting again in Theatre.

The swing doors closed behind the surgeon, but Mark stayed. Lucy shut her eyes and tried to concentrate. 'Mark, what happened before I fell out of the tree? You ... were angry with me about something, but I can't remember what it was.'

He sat down beside her. 'It's unimportant, my dear girl. Forget it,' but she worried away at the subject until Caroline appeared, still in her theatre garb of green dress and head-scarf.

'What a thing to do, Lucy! You've nearly frightened poor William to death. Thank heavens for you, Mark!' and she gripped his hand hard.

'I'll leave you girls to it, then.' Mark glanced at his watch. 'You'll be in Theatre in a few minutes, Lucy, and when you wake up again you'll feel quite different.'

She didn't feel much better, though she was less muddled, when she came round in a small side ward. Her body ached all over, and her right leg felt stiff and uncomfortable, suspended by a complicated sling and pulley system from an overhead beam. The blood transfusion was still dripping slowly into her arm.

'You were bleeding internally,' Caroline told her later that evening. She regarded her sister soberly. 'If William hadn't come back when he did . . .' She left it at that, but Lucy knew what she had nearly said. Caroline thought that she was lucky to be alive. She could have bled to death, unable to move because of her broken leg, her life ebbing away under the hot August sun. Lucy shivered and her mouth felt dry. Oh, it was good to be alive, even if things weren't always as you wanted them. Even if—'Mark!' she thought. 'I quarrelled with Mark!' And this time she remembered what it had been about.

'Oh, Mark,' she whispered, unaware that Caroline had heard her, and two tears rolled down her pale cheeks on to the pillow.

Caroline bent over her, concerned and uncertain. 'What is it, Lucy? What was that about Mark?'

'We had a row about something, Caro. Just before I fell out of the tree.'

'It couldn't have been a very serious row.' Caroline sounded amused now. 'Mark's been an absolute tower of strength, keeping William calm, telephoning Father and Susan. They'll be back tomorrow morning. Mark insisted there was no need for them to rush home tonight. William is going to sleep at his place, and Kevin says he can look after himself.'

'Oh, my goodness, Caro! I'd quite forgotten about the visitors. There are three people arriving tomorrow evening.' Lucy tried to sit up in her agitation, but fell back against the pillows.

Caroline laid a soothing hand on her forehead. 'It's all right, darling. Honestly! Mrs Rudge's daughter is going to help out for a few days.'

'But she's got a family. And they're only little.'

'She'll run the house and Susan will look after the children. Good practice if she really does become an au pair girl.'

Lucy gave a weak giggle, because one of Susan's ambitions was to be an au pair girl to the family of a Greek shipping magnate. 'Who knows,' she would say airily, 'I might marry one of his relations!'

They were all amused by Susan's daydreams. Lucy sobered to ask a little uneasily, 'Has anyone told her?'

'Not yet,' Caroline smiled, 'but if she's offered the alternative of cooking and housework, I know which she'll choose! And she's quite good with children, so you're not to worry. Everything's under control.'

However, Lucy did worry, because these were only temporary measures, and what would happen if Mrs Green could only stay a few days? If they put off the visitors who were booked for the next month, they would lose money, while even if they found someone to run the house they would lose money anyway, for the wages would eat into their profits.

'Can't you sleep, dear?' asked the night nurse, who had been detailed to take Lucy's pulse half-hourly. 'Time for your next injection, then.'

As the morphia took effect Lucy's problems seemed to melt away. Somehow they would manage. Somehow she would make it up with Mark.

'Mark . . . I wish you would come,' she murmured, and drifted off to sleep.

The only visitors she was allowed next morning were her father and Susan, who stayed no more than ten minutes, repeated Caroline's words, that she was not to worry about the house, and left, as they put it, to get on with the job. Dr Berrington arrived at eleven, accompanied by the orthopaedic consultant. They explained to Lucy that she had fractured her femur, and that the slings and pulleys attached to her leg were only a temporary arrangement.

'As soon as you're fit enough I shall operate on your leg,' the orthopaedic man explained. 'Put a nail down the shaft to hold the bone together. You'll be mobile much quicker than you would be on traction only.'

Lucy didn't like the sound of a nail in her leg, but anything that got her on her feet more quickly could be endured somehow.

'It's standard procedure,' Caroline informed her, when she called in later. 'They would have done it at the same time as the other op if they'd thought you were up to it.'

'Was I really that bad?'

'Practically exsanguinated,' Caroline told her cheerfully. 'They sucked pints out of your abdominal cavity!'

Lucy shuddered and turned her face away.

'You've a lot to learn about handling patients, Caroline,' a sardonic voice said from the doorway. 'You'll get a bad reputation if you frighten them to death!'

Lucy looked round quickly. Mark came in, shutting the door behind him.

Caroline looked remorseful. 'I'm truly sorry, Lucy. I forgot you're not medical.'

'Even if she was I doubt she'd want to hear the grisly details about her own case,' Mark said drily, coming to the edge of the bed to stare down at Lucy. 'How are you, little one?'

'All right,' whispered Lucy, overcome by shyness now that she remembered the scene in the orchard. So much had happened since then. It was hard to believe it was less than forty-eight hours ago.

'Sister says you didn't have a very good night. She thinks you're worrying about something.'

'Yes, the house,' Caroline interposed, 'though we've told her everything's under control.'

'Not the house,' Lucy said tiredly. 'It's ... the things we said to each other, Mark. I don't like quarrelling with you.' She blinked hard to keep the tears away.

Mark was silent for so long that she looked up at him anxiously, to find him staring at her with a curious expression on his face. There was affection there, no doubt about it—and a hint of regret.

'I'm sorry, Lucy,' he said quietly. 'The fault was entirely

mine. You were quite right, I shouldn't have interfered. How you run your life is your own affair.'

'Well, well!' exclaimed Caroline, wide-eyed with curiosity. 'What a touching little scene! Mind telling me what it's all about?'

'Yes, I do,' Mark said bluntly. 'This is between your sister and me, so just keep out of it.' He tempered his words with a half-smile, then touched Lucy lightly on the shoulder. 'I mustn't stop. Sister issued strict orders.'

'I should have thought that a consultant made his own rules,' Caroline observed.

He shook his head. 'Consultants have to set a good example, Caroline.'

As he turned away Lucy tried to stop him. 'But Mark, I—I haven't explained. About yesterday—you got the wrong idea——'

'My dear girl,' he said gently, 'yesterday is over. I'd prefer to forget about it.' He clamped a hand on Caroline's shoulder and turned her towards the door. 'Your sister looks worn out. Let's leave her in peace.'

After they had gone Lucy felt thoroughly miserable. Mark was being kind and considerate because he was a doctor, and he knew how important peace of mind was to a patient's recovery. Or perhaps he was bored with the whole incident, and annoyed with himself for reacting so strongly to her affairs. Why *had* he been angry? Lucy wondered, drawing what comfort she could from the thought that at least he must care for her a little, or he would not have lost his temper so completely.

CHAPTER TEN

SMOOTHLY, efficiently, the hospital machine took over Lucy's life, absorbing her completely into its routine. Ward rounds, drug rounds, bedtime when she felt awake, breakfast when she would have preferred to sleep, visitors when Sister said she could have them. One or other of the family looked in every afternoon, and assured her that the house was running smoothly. Mrs Rudge's daughter was enjoying herself and hinted that she wouldn't mind staying on until Lucy was fit again.

'But who will look after her children when you go back to school?' Lucy asked Susan, and Susan gave an impish smile.

'I don't have to go back to school. I've got quite a decent set of O-levels.'

They had been better than anyone had expected, and her father had told Lucy about them only yesterday. 'Of course you should go back,' said Lucy. 'You ought to try for A-levels.'

Susan shook her head. 'I don't want to go in the Sixth Form. I'd rather help with the kids until you're better, and then I'll decide what I want to do. I wouldn't mind a year abroad soaking up the sun.'

'Au pairs don't lie on the beach all day.'

Susan smiled pityingly, 'I know that, silly, but they do have some rights.'

'And some restrictions,' Lucy warned. 'I don't believe anyone would take you until you're at least seventeen.'

'Which will be in November,' Susan pointed out. 'And you won't be able to work before then, so what are we arguing about?'

Lucy hadn't expected to be out of action so long. She

145

hadn't asked, and no one had told her, the time it took broken bones to unite.

When pressed that evening Caroline agreed that Susan's information was correct. 'But it could be longer if you're unlucky,' her sister warned her. 'Though Dr Carter says you're splendidly healthy. He plans to operate any day now.'

'Yes, I know. He told me this morning.' The orthopaedic surgeon had visited her again with Dr Berrington, who had professed himself well pleased with her progress. 'I wish I didn't have to go through it all again,' Lucy added with a sigh. 'It's not the operation itself, it's afterwards you feel so rotten.'

'That's because you were so shocked. This is what we call a cold case, delayed until you're completely fit. Honestly, Lucy, there's nothing to worry about.'

Her sister was not the only young doctor to call in. Henry came, and Kevin Cassidy, Chris Stevens and several others. Lucy was pleased to see them, but longed for one visitor who didn't come again. In the end she was forced to ask Caroline about him.

'Is Mark away? He hasn't been in lately.'

'I expect he's busy,' Caroline said carelessly. 'And with Camilla around——'

'Camilla? I thought she was in London.'

'Didn't I tell you?' Caroline fiddled with her hair in Lucy's mirror. She wore it in a softer, more feminine style these days because Henry liked it that way. 'She's given up the London job.'

Lucy's hands clenched and her breath came more quickly. She stared at her sister's back, watched Caroline shrug into the white coat that she had discarded on arrival. 'Don't go, Caro. Please stay a bit longer.'

'I'm sorry, but I have to write up some progress notes for tomorrow's ward round.'

'Caro, please—do you mean that—that they're getting married?'

Caroline stared. 'What are you on about? Oh, Mark and Camilla! I don't know. Don't care either, I'm glad to say!' She hung in the doorway for a moment, smiling at her past foolishness. 'I must have been mad, drooling on about Mark. He's not my type at all really. Perhaps Henry and I will make it to the altar before they do.'

She waved an airy hand in farewell and departed to the wards, a girl transformed by love. The edginess, the self-absorption were both gone, thanks to nice Henry Wilson and his quiet persistence. He was one of Lucy's favourite visitors, because he was so relaxing.

When she told him this he gave his gentle smile and shook his head ruefully. 'I'm not feeling very relaxed just now. Not since I heard the news about Miss Fielding.' When she asked him what he meant he shook his head again and sighed heavily. 'Hasn't Caroline told you? She's standing in for one of our anaesthetists, who's going off to the States for a month or two. She'll be my immediate boss, worse luck. I am not an admirer of the lady, though Caroline seems to like her.'

'You mean . . . she's already here?'

He said gloomily that indeed she was. She had started two days ago. 'Don't get me wrong. She's first class at her job, but she has a sharp tongue, and she's not very tolerant of her juniors' mistakes.'

'How odd,' murmured Lucy. 'I thought she wanted the job in London because it was vital to her career.'

Henry shrugged. 'Perhaps she decided that her career was less important than her fiancé.'

Lucy asked the question that Caroline had been unable to answer, colouring a little and hoping Henry didn't notice. 'Do you know when they're getting married?'

But Henry had no idea either, and seemed no more interested than Caroline had been. 'Not much point when she's so busy. With one consultant away and another on holiday, we're all covering extra sessions.'

As a result of Henry's news Lucy was less surprised

than she might have been when Camilla Fielding walked
into her room that afternoon, accompanied by Sister. That
it was an official visit was at once apparent. Camilla had on a
well cut and superbly laundered white coat, not at all like
the regulation hospital issue worn by Caroline and Henry.
She was brisk, efficient and coolly pleasant.

'Did I wake you up, Miss Grant? I just want a quick look
at you before tomorrow's operation.'

Sister was by the bed, helping Lucy off with her night-
dress. Camilla's stethoscope began to move methodically
over Lucy's chest.

'Blood pressure now, Sister.' As she wound the cuff
round Lucy's arm, Lucy stared into her impassive face.

'I thought ... doctors didn't do things on ... on people
they know.'

'Not on friends, no,' Camilla agreed calmly, 'but we
hardly know each other, dear.' She put the stethoscope ends
in her ears and lowered her head. 'Don't talk now, please.'
She folded the cuff up again and said briskly, 'That's fine.
You've got over the chest infection you had after your
operation. Not nervous about tomorrow?'

'Yes, I am,' muttered Lucy. 'I've been on edge since
they told me. Is it really necessary?'

'Of course it is. You don't think a busy man like Dr
Carter would waste his time on an unnecessary operation?'
As Camilla looked down at Lucy's tense face her own
softened. 'There really is nothing to worry about,' she
added more kindly. 'And you'll be on your feet much
quicker than if they left you slung up on this apparatus,'
and she gestured at Lucy's suspended leg.

Caroline and Henry looked in last thing at night to cheer
her up before her coming ordeal.

'I wish I wasn't having Dr Fielding,' Lucy told them.

They both expressed surprise. 'She's good at her job,'
said Henry.

'And very decent really, once you get to know her.'

'She doesn't like me,' Lucy said unhappily. 'She should

have asked someone else to take my case.'

They looked at one another and laughed. 'Doctors on duty don't allow personal feelings to intrude.'

'Mark said he would never operate on a friend.'

'That's rather different. He knows you well; Camilla doesn't.'

'But if you don't like someone——'

'Lucy dear,' Henry said firmly, taking her hand in a tight grip, 'you're not suggesting that Camilla is going to give you an overdose, I hope?' He made a joke of it and Lucy smiled weakly. 'That's better,' he went on. 'You have a splendid surgeon and a first class anaesthetist, so you have absolutely nothing to worry about.'

'I know that really. Have you s-seen Mark today?'

'Yes, I have. Why, Lucy?'

'Oh, nothing.' She turned her face into the pillow. 'Just that I'd—I'd have liked to see him. I'm a bit tired now, I think I'll go to sleep.'

Caroline bent down and rather surprisingly kissed her on the forehead. 'Cheer up, it'll soon be over,' but there was concern on her face as she went out with Henry.

The night nurse was settling Lucy a short time later, when there was a brisk rap on the door and Mark walked in. The main light was off, and he stood in shadow, so that she couldn't see his face clearly.

'Caroline said you wanted to see me?' There was a query in his voice.

Very conscious of the night nurse, who was shifting things on her bedside locker, Lucy mumbled incoherently. Mark advanced to her side. 'What is it, little one?'

'You . . . didn't come in specially?' Lucy asked foolishly, and he smiled down at her.

'I was looking at a patient. I met Caroline in the common-room. If you could give us two minutes alone, Staff?'

The staff nurse said doubtfully, 'Miss Grant's supposed to have an early night, sir.'

'I said two minutes.' Mark put his hands on the girl's

shoulders and turned her towards the door. 'Go and find someone else to fuss over,' he said pleasantly but firmly, and the nurse, looking outraged, went out of the room.

Lucy gave a weak giggle. 'Oh, Mark, you've made her cross!'

'Rubbish!' He hooked a chair forward and sat down beside her. 'Now tell me what's wrong.'

'Nothing's wrong, honestly. I'm sorry Caro bothered you. I—I just happened to say that—that I hadn't seen you for some time.' In spite of herself there was reproach in her voice.

Mark stared at her very hard. 'And you missed me, Lucy? I find that difficult to believe.'

She swallowed nervously, her hands clenched tightly on the sheets. 'Well, I did. I thought you might—might still be annoyed with me.'

He frowned and shook his head irritably. 'I've told you already, I prefer to forget that stupid business. It didn't reflect very creditably on either of us.'

'I know,' whispered Lucy, miserably because he didn't want to listen, 'But—but what I said to you, Mark——'

'Oh, for God's sake!' he exploded 'can't you drop it? You're a big girl now. Run your life how you please, though you can't expect me to approve.'

'I don't think you have any right to be so high and mighty!' Lucy snapped, furious because he wouldn't let her explain.

'What does that mean?' Mark asked quietly, but with an alarmingly grim expression that Lucy was too worked up to notice.

'I mean you and Camilla, of course. Everyone knows you live together, so what right have you to criticise me? Not that there's anything——'

His hand clamped on her arm so hard that she winced. 'Be quiet, Lucy,' he grated. 'Camilla and I are engaged. We plan to get married. I take it you aren't expecting Cassidy to marry you?' This with sarcasm. When she remained silent he added heavily, 'I hope not at any rate, because if you are you'll be disappointed.'

The door started to open, and Mark took his hand away quickly, just as the Night Superintendant came in, accompanied by the staff nurse. 'Mr Franklin, I really must ask you to go now.' The Night Superintendant was dignified and purposeful, and Mark, lips compressed, nodded irritably.

'I'm just off.' He looked down at Lucy. 'I think, my dear girl, it would have been better if I'd stayed away.' He said this under his breath, so that the waiting women couldn't possibly have heard, but they stared as he passed them, aware of tension in the air. At the door he paused for a moment.

'Good luck tomorrow,' he said quietly, and went out.

The Night Superintendant watched while Lucy was settled down, saw her take the two white tablets that Staff Nurse gave her. 'We want you to have a good sleep before the big day!'

She wouldn't sleep, Lucy thought miserably, because Mark was too much on her mind. If only she hadn't said those silly things to him about Kevin and herself! If only he would listen when she tried to explain. If only she hadn't lost her head just now and made those idiotic remarks about him and Camilla. She rubbed the sore place on her arm where Mark's fingers had dug into her. The fierceness of his grip was an indication of how much she had angered him.

'Oh, Mark,' she whispered forlornly, and the tears slid down her cheeks, so that she had to fumble for a paper tissue to wipe them away.

'We want you to have a good sleep,' the night nurse had said. Lucy turned away from the dim light that percolated through the glass partition in the door. She didn't expect to sleep for hours, but the tablets were potent and did their work effectively. When the staff nurse looked in an hour later she was sleeping soundly, and didn't wake until morning.

They wheeled her into the operating theatre at nine o'clock. In the anaesthetic room Dr Carter spoke to her for a moment, briskly and cheerfully, telling her she would be as good as new in a few months.

'I don't fancy walking around with ironmongery in my leg,' Lucy sighed, drowsy with her premedication.

He laughed and told her they would take it out later. Then he was gone and Camilla appeared, wearing a green theatre dress, with her hair completely hidden under a green head-scarf. She looked impressively efficient as she bent over the anaesthetic trolley, filling her syringes, checking on the gas cylinders. She had smiled at Lucy when she came in, quite an ordinary friendly smile, which Lucy returned rather waveringly. The nurse who was assisting rolled back the sleeve of Lucy's theatre gown, and Camilla twisted a soft piece of rubber tubing round her arm.

'I don't want an anaesthetic, thank you,' Lucy said clearly and politely, but oddly it sounded as if her words came from a great distance away.

Camilla sat down on one of the theatre stools and laid a cool hand on Lucy's wrist. Lucy eyed the syringe apprehensively, and Henry's words came back to her. 'You're not suggesting that Camilla's going to give you an overdose?'

Panic swept over her. She struggled to sit up, and the nurse moved quickly to restrain her.

'She has been premedicated?' Camilla asked sharply, and the nurse, looking flustered, said that she must have been.

'Must?' snapped Camilla. 'Don't you know? Then check with the ward nurse.'

The ward nurse was in the corridor. As the theatre nurse went out quickly, Lucy eyed Camilla apprehensively. 'How do I know what you're giving me? You could easily see that I don't come round again.'

Her words tailed off at the look on Camilla's face—blank incredulity, then annoyance, then a sort of irritated amusement.

'Don't be a complete fool, my dear.' She was spared further words by the return of the theatre nurse, with the ward nurse close behind.

'Sorry, doctor, I couldn't find a pair of shoes. Of course she's been premedicated.'

She was a nice friendly girl, and she held Lucy's hand, murmuring soothing words, though it wasn't really necessary now. Lucy knew that she had behaved ridiculously. Camilla might not like her, but she was a dedicated doctor. She would never allow her personal feelings to intrude on her professional work; the idea was preposterous. So Lucy shut her eyes and didn't need the soft-spoken request to keep still. She felt the small prick on the back of her hand, heard the murmur of voices, tried to say she was sorry, but got no further than the first word.

She felt very ashamed of herself when she remembered the incident next day. Camilla came in, as anaesthetists do, to check that her chest was all right after the anaesthetic. Lucy submitted to her examination in silence. Camilla returned her stethoscope to the pocket of her white coat, and gave an approving nod to the nurse in attendance.

'Sounds fine. How are you feeling, Lucy?' It was one of the few times she had called Lucy by her first name.

'I'm feeling an awful fool, if you want the truth, Dr Fielding.'

Camilla's well-shaped eyebrows rose. She extended a slim white hand and inspected her nails. Mark's ring glittered on her third finger. 'Let's be kind and say you were a bit disorientated,' she suggested. 'People react in odd ways sometimes to drugs. You were more than a little ... confused.' There was a glimmer of humour in the clear blue eyes, but whether she was laughing at or with the other girl, Lucy couldn't decide.

'Anyway, I'm sorry,' she mumbled. 'I . . . hope you won't tell Mark.'

Camilla's smile vanished. 'How you do go on about Mark! I shouldn't dream of boring him with such a stupid story.'

As she swept out the staff nurse lingered for a moment and pulled a hideous face behind Camilla's back. 'Bitch,' she mouthed, then shut the door quickly as Camilla's voice rang out.

'Hurry up, Staff. We've two more patients to see.'

Once she had got used to being idle, Lucy had to admit that she felt better for the rest. The three years since her mother had died had been hectic and demanding, and the last four months the most strenuous of all. It was a relief to pass over the responsibility for running the house into the capable hands of Mrs Rudge's daughter, even though the profits they were making were much smaller.

'But it won't be for long, love,' Mrs Rudge assured her, when she called one afternoon with a bunch of roses and a box of chocolate peppermint creams.

'You are kind,' said Lucy, 'but you didn't have to bring anything.'

'Bless you, dear, I like to do it. Your mum was that kind to me when I had my own operation!' Mrs Rudge cast an eye round the small room and waved the flowers in her hand. 'I needn't have brought these, certainly. You do have a lot of admirers.'

Lucy smiled a little self-consciously, for Chris had brought in carnations and roses, a bunch of grapes, a pile of magazines. Kevin had given her the latest thriller, which was tough and cynical, and not at all to Lucy's taste. Henry, who understood her better, had lent her a life of Sir Thomas Beecham and told her smilingly that since they would soon be related, he believed in getting on her right side!

'It's because of Caro,' Lucy explained. 'The residents all know me through her.'

Mrs Rudge had never liked Caroline. 'Nothing to do with your sister,' she commented. 'They like you because you're a very pretty and nice young girl. And you look absolutely sweet in that nightie, love. I'm not surprised you have hordes of visitors.'

'You're good for my morale, Mrs Rudge! Tell me all the local news, will you?'

There was nothing Mrs Rudge liked better than a good gossip. When she had filled Lucy in on last weekend's village wedding, and the row that was going on over who should do what for the church fête, she drew breath for a moment before embarking on a new theme.

'You know that Mr Franklin, who used to live with you? A friend of mine is cleaning for him.'

'Really?' murmured Lucy. 'I hope his house is in order by now?'

'I don't know about that,' said Mrs Rudge, 'but Molly likes working for them.'

'Them? You mean——' Lucy was faintly surprised that Mark and Camilla were living together openly, since she had a vague idea that doctors liked to cultivate at least an image of respectability!

'Mr Franklin and his mother,' Mrs Rudge added. 'A very charming lady, Molly says.'

This news made Lucy thoughtful. Unless Mrs Franklin was an unusual parent, it was hard to imagine her approving of the way Mark and Camilla conducted their affairs. Or perhaps she didn't approve, but wanted to keep her son's friendship.

'Where is Camilla staying while she works here?' Lucy asked Henry and Caroline, on their next visit.

'In a hospital apartment,' Caroline answered. 'Why?'

'I just wondered,' said Lucy, colouring slightly. 'Mrs Rudge told me Mark's mother is staying with him.'

Henry and Caroline were not very interested in the Franklins' affairs, being more concerned with their own. Caroline finished her present job in a month's time, and was wondering whether to apply for Mark's. Henry wanted her to take several months off, so that they could get married and at least begin their life together without the problems created by two demanding careers.

Lucy could see that Caroline was weakening. 'Henry's right,' she told her sister. 'Putting your career first doesn't seem to make for happiness. Look at Mark and Camilla. They don't strike me as a very happy couple.'

'How you do go on about those two,' Caroline remarked, looking at her sister rather quizzically, and Henry said that in his opinion that twosome wasn't going to last much longer.

Caroline disagreed. 'She gave up that job in London for Mark. Does that sound as if they're about to break up?'

Henry shrugged and the talk returned to their own affairs, so Lucy was reduced to attempting to extract news from William. He was back at school now and came in most days on his way home. Lucy led up to the important question in a roundabout way.

'You don't have time to go over to Mark's place now, I suppose?'

'No, I don't.'

'Had his mother arrived when you were still going?'

'Yes.'

'What's she like?'

William rummaged through a box of chocolates brought in by Kevin. 'All right,' he said at last.

These were typical William replies. Lucy tried again. 'Do you know how long she's staying?'

'No idea.'

'Do Camilla and she get on?'

William stared at her in astonishment. 'Honestly, Luce! How should I know? What's got into you? I hate nosey people!' He looked at his watch, his young face rigid with disapproval. 'Time I was off, I've a lot to study tonight.'

Next day Lucy had her stitches out, an uncomfortable

process, but a sure sign of progress. The physiotherapists had started to work on her before this, but now at Dr Carter's decree they spent longer on her each day.

'When shall I be able to go home?' was Lucy's constantly recurring question, and Dr Carter's stock reply was, 'It's early days yet. Be patient a little longer.'

It was hard to be patient when you had always been an active person, and doubly hard when you were eating your heart out for someone who never came. Lucy had given up hoping for another visit from Mark; the last one had been so disastrous that it was understandable he would not want to repeat it. Not that she was short of visitors. A procession of young doctors made their way to Lucy's room, Kevin and Chris and a dozen others, besides the older men who had been friends of her parents.

Chris had changed to Mark's team, so his visits were especially welcome. If she couldn't see the man she loved, the next best thing was hearing about him, and Chris mentioned him a great deal. The young house surgeon admired and respected his new chief, though he was still a good deal in awe of him.

'Franklin can be horribly abrasive if you do the wrong thing,' he remarked, and told Lucy about a minor misdemeanour he had committed, something to do with a mislaid X-ray form. 'Mind, it *was* important,' he admitted with a sigh, 'but he was angrier than I'd have expected. He's been more edgy than usual lately. We've all noticed it.'

Something to do with Camilla? Or his mother's visit? 'Have you met Mrs Franklin?' Lucy asked, but of course Chris hadn't. She was not very likely to frequent the residents' quarters, though she might be curious to see the hospital where her son worked.

That was how Lucy met her in the end. She was walking with crutches now, and every afternoon she would make her slow and laborious way up and down the main corridor, the physiotherapist by her side. And every time she saw a tall white-coated figure in the distance she would long for it to be Mark, but every time she was disappointed.

Then one Tuesday afternoon, when she had almost given up hope, a side door on the corridor opened and footsteps sounded behind them. A woman spoke and a man answered, a man who spoke abruptly, who sounded exactly like Mark. Lucy froze on her crutches, her heart beating wildly. She would not—she would not turn round, but her breath was coming jerkily and her arms felt weak.

'Are you all right?' the physiotherapist asked concernedly. 'You're looking rather pale.'

'I'm ... feeling a bit tired,' Lucy said untruthfully.

The footsteps were right behind them now. 'Hallo, Lucy,' said Mark. 'Glad to see you on your feet again.'

She rested heavily on her crutches and could think of absolutely nothing to say. The middle-aged woman beside Mark was regarding her with a sympathetic smile.

'Mother, this is Lucy Grant, whose house I lived in when I first came to Barnslow.'

'I remember, dear.' Mrs Franklin extended a hand, realised Lucy couldn't shake it and gave an apologetic smile. 'How silly of me, Lucy! It must be very awkward for you on those things.'

Mrs Rudge's friend was right, thought Lucy; Mark's mother was charming. She had his fine grey eyes and the same very direct way of looking at you, but her manner was gentle, kindly, relaxed, and she seemed in no hurry to move on. She wanted to know what had caused Lucy's accident? How much longer Lucy would be in hospital? Who was running the house while Lucy was away?

'So worrying for you, dear,' she said sympathetically, and Mark shifted impatiently in the background.

'Mother, we *are* supposed to be meeting Camilla at four. See you some time, Lucy.'

They walked on, rapidly outstripping Lucy and the physiotherapist, the tall man and the elegant middle-aged woman, perfectly dressed in a well cut linen suit, whose subtle shade of lavender complemented her pretty grey hair. She had the figure of a girl and long slender legs. Her step was as light as Mark's and her face had been almost unlined.

'What a beautiful woman,' observed Lucy's companion.

'Yes, she is. And nice too.' And kindly, which Mark was not.

There had been no warmth in his greeting. After that brief introduction he had stood back, looking bored and supercilious. It was very evident that he had washed his hands of Lucy Grant entirely.

CHAPTER ELEVEN

THE day after this encounter Sister looked into Lucy's room while she was having her afternoon tea. 'You've had your physio session, Miss Grant? Good. There's a visitor for you,' and to Lucy's surprise Mrs Franklin walked in a few moments later.

'I should have come before if I'd known about your accident. I can't think why Mark didn't mention it.'

'There was really no reason why he should,' Lucy answered. 'We don't see each other often these days.'

The older woman sat down opposite her and regarded her pleasantly. 'There was every reason why he should. I've been wanting to meet you ever since I came down, my dear.'

'Really?' said Lucy, rather at a loss. If Mrs Franklin had wanted to meet her, she could have found out from Mark where she was.

'Yes, really.' Mark's mother smiled very sweetly. 'I wanted to thank you for looking after my son so well.'

'It was nothing,' muttered Lucy. 'I just treated him the same as everyone else.'

Mrs Franklin shook her head. 'You made him very comfortable. You made him feel at home. Which is why I'm so cross with him. When I said I would like to meet you, he told me you weren't at home. Not a word about your accident. I find my son very difficult to understand!'

Lucy said that Mark was very busy, which sometimes made him absentminded. A silly remark, to which Mrs Franklin responded with a sceptical look.

'He could hardly have forgotten you were in hospital! I hope you won't be offended, my dear, but is there some reason for Mark's odd behaviour? He used to speak about you so warmly when he wrote, and I couldn't help noticing that yesterday——' she hesitated, choosing her words carefully—'yesterday he seemed positively unfriendly.'

Lucy bit her lip and avoided the other woman's eyes. Mrs Franklin studied her unhappy young face with a look of genuine concern. 'I'm sorry, Lucy. Forgive me for interfering.'

'No, it's all right.' Suddenly Lucy wanted to talk. It would be a relief to unburden herself, especially to such a sympathetic listener, provided that she was careful and didn't give too much away. So it all came out, their initial disapproval of each other ('Though I'm sure it was my fault as much as his'), their growing friendship, Mark's tendency to interfere.

'He does just the same with me,' Mark's mother commented amusedly.

Lucy even told her about the incident with the whisky, and how kind Mark had been to her father, though she skirted round the reason for his departure. 'And then, after he left, everything went wrong,' she ended forlornly. 'He—he didn't approve of one of my friends. I told him it was none of his business, and it ended with us having a really horrible row.' She was pleating the skirt of her dressing-gown nervously, and the older woman's face was full of concern.

'I begin to understand. How typical of Mark! Throwing his weight about, losing his temper.'

'I lost mine too,' Lucy admitted.

'I'm sure you did, you poor child. And who could blame you? My son is the absolute limit!' At Lucy's startled expression she smiled again. 'You don't think a mother should be so disloyal? I'm devoted to Mark, but I'm quite aware of his faults.'

'But in a sense it was *my* fault that we quarrelled,' Lucy said slowly, and because she had already told Mrs Franklin so much the rest came out quite easily—the trip with Kevin, the way she had allowed Mark to think that Kevin and she were having an affair. 'It was such a stupid thing to do,' she ended unhappily, 'but he was so—so disapproving—and—and dictatorial. I wasn't going to let him tell me how to run my life. I suppose I wanted to assert my independence.'

Mrs Franklin laughed, but her glance was thoughtful as she studied Lucy's bent head. 'You're looking tired, my dear. I think I should go now.' She leant forward and laid a slim white hand over Lucy's brown one. 'I should like to come and see you again if I may? I shall be staying with Mark for quite a time.'

After she had gone Lucy lay back in her comfortable chair by the open window, and stared out at the misty September sunshine. Her room overlooked the hospital garden, which was a source of great pleasure to her. She felt more relaxed than she had been for weeks. Mark's mother was a good listener. She had understood, because she understood her son. It would be nice to see her again, if she really intended to come, and Lucy didn't think Mrs Franklin said things she didn't mean. She shut her eyes, enjoying the sun on her face. Would Mrs Franklin mention her visit to Mark? It seemed likely. He would probably not approve; he might even be annoyed. He would certainly not have liked Lucy's detailed account of their progression from friendship to their present strained relationship.

There was one person Lucy had avoided mentioning, and that was Camilla. If Mrs Franklin had noticed this omission she hadn't commented on it, nor had she probed into Lucy's rather confused account of her quarrel with Mark. But she had listened very intently and perhaps she would tell Mark the truth, that he was imagining more between Kevin and Lucy than really existed. And perhaps Mark would believe her.

She met him again the next time the physiotherapist took her down the main corridor. It was so long that people at the far end were small and unrecognisable. As Lucy made her slow and laboured way, she saw a crowd of people emerge from one of the wards at the far end. They walked rapidly towards her, and she strained her eyes to see if Mark was among them. Half a dozen white-coated figures, the one in the centre taller than the rest. A familiar stride. A dark head. She could see his face and it *was* Mark, going round the wards with his juniors, for he was turning into Female Surgical now. Chris Stevens was holding the ward door open for his chief.

Mark saw Lucy approaching and halted for a moment, watching critically as she advanced towards him. 'You ought to be managing better than that,' he said severely, and to the physiotherapist, 'Keep her at it! She's inclined to be lazy!'

At Lucy's indignant look he added crisply, 'Joke, my dear girl. You're quite revoltingly energetic when you're at home. Don't you agree, Stevens?' Chris smiled and nodded. 'You go on, boys,' Mark added. 'I'll be with you in a minute.' He waved them into the ward and walked over to Lucy. 'My mother told me about her visit. You seem to have covered a lot of ground in a short time.'

Lucy looked up into his unsmiling face and wished that they were alone. The physiotherapist, perhaps sensing this, moved away tactfully. 'I like your mother, Mark. She was very kind to me.'

'She likes you too,' Mark said briskly. 'She's entirely on your side.' The grey eyes that were so like his mother's stared down at her.

'Is there any question of sides?'

'Oh, definitely.' His voice had sharpened. 'She thinks your complaints about me are fully justified.'

Lucy's grip tightened on her crutches. 'I didn't complain, Mark—honestly. I just told her the truth.' Beneath his sceptical and unfriendly gaze her colour deepened. 'I would like you to believe what I told her,' she added quietly, 'but if you won't there's nothing I can do about it.'

He shrugged as if he wasn't very interested. 'Shall we drop the matter, Lucy?' and as she turned away, 'Just one more thing. My mother talks too much, when she's with someone she likes. Probably because she's alone a good deal since my father died. I should bear it in mind if I were you.'

'I think that's unkind,' Lucy retorted. 'Your mother's a dear and we get on very well.' She moved away from him and the physiotherapist joined her. A jolly girl, with scant respect for her superiors, she screwd up her face and jerked her head at the swing door Mark had just walked through. 'Tough customer, isn't he? I wouldn't care to get on the wrong side of that one.'

Lucy ploughed on, past a row of interested men patients, sitting on a bench outside their ward. 'It sounded as if he was telling you off,' the girl persisted. 'Do you know him well?'

'Quite well,' Lucy said shortly. Well enough to love, she thought miserably, totally unaware of the soft whistle the youngest of the watching men had given.

The physiotherapist, who was not, gave a self-conscious giggle, and in the ensuing badinage dropped the subject, greatly to Lucy's relief.

Another day she met Camilla. Although she was still on her own in the small single-bed side ward, she liked to meet the other patients in the day room. She was sitting in there one afternoon when Camilla came in, stethoscope in hand, accompanied by the staff nurse on duty.

'Would you mind examining Mrs Preece in here, doctor,' the staff nurse said apologetically. 'Her bed's just been stripped.'

Camilla nodded and the nurse moved a couple of patients, so that she could put screens round Mrs Preece's chair. While she was doing this Camilla exchanged a few words with Lucy.

'I hear you're going home soon, Miss Grant.'

'That's right, Dr Fielding.'

'Good,' Camilla said graciously. 'Do hurry up, Staff! I'm already behind.'

Staff Nurse, looking flustered, was shouting instructions at deaf old Mrs Preece. 'Your cardigan off, dear, and your nightie unbuttoned! Doctor wants to examine your chest.'

Camilla, looking irritated, moved behind the screens. The nurse had forgotten the blood pressure machine. She rushed out, tripped over a patient's foot, and skidded across the floor.

'Clumsy idiot!' snapped Camilla.

'Who's Lady Muck?' asked one of Lucy's companions, and someone else said, 'That's one of the anaesthetists.'

'Glad she didn't do me,' the first woman retorted, and Camilla poked her head round the screen crossly.

'Would you please be quiet, all of you. I'm trying to listen to this patient's chest.'

Into the ensuing silence, Staff Nurse, returning with the sphygmomanometer, announced to Lucy, 'There's a visitor for you, Miss Grant—Mrs Franklin.'

Camilla, who had already disappeared behind the screens again, pulled one open to stare at Lucy. 'Mrs Franklin?' she queried. 'Not *Mark's* mother?' and when Lucy nodded, 'I didn't know you two had even met.'

Lucy struggled to her feet, helped by another patient. 'She came to see me recently. It's very kind of her to bother.'

'Very kind,' Camilla agreed, and most peculiar her tone implied. 'Well, come on, come on, Staff! Get her sleeve rolled up!'

Leaving the unfortunate staff nurse to cope with a short-tempered doctor and a muddled old lady, Lucy made her way down the ward and into her own room. Mrs Franklin, looking delightfully pretty in a fine wool dress of softest blue, rose smilingly from her chair.

'I'm glad you're making such good progress, my dear.' She gestured towards a small parcel on the bed. 'You have so many flowers and more fruit than you can possibly eat! I thought a book might be more acceptable.'

Lucy unwrapped the paper, touched by her thoughtfulness. It was a paperback edition of the memoirs of a famous singer.

'If you've read it the shop will change it.'

Lucy turned the pages over happily. 'I haven't, but I've always wanted to. How did you know I was interested in music?'

'Mark told me. He also told me that you had to give up your own career to look after your family.' They talked a little about that, and then about music in general, and Lucy was delighted to discover that Mark's mother was a keen amateur musician, who played the piano and sang in her local choral society. They were swapping musical stories, sitting close together and totally absorbed, when there was a knock on the door and Camilla looked in.

'Still here, Aunt Beth? Would you give Mark a message for me? Tell him I won't be free until nine.' Her eyes moved from Mrs Franklin to Lucy, then back again. 'I'm just going to tea. Perhaps you'd like some, Aunt Beth?'

Mrs Franklin shook her head. 'Thank you, Camilla, but I've already had a cup with Lucy. I'll pass on your message to Mark.'

Behind Mrs Franklin's back Camilla stared at Lucy, her expression unfriendly. 'See you later, then,' she said at last, and she shut the door with a little bang.

Lucy had the distinct impression that Camilla had manufactured a message so that she could look in on them, for if Mark had already left the hospital she could have rung him at home. She had wanted to see if Mrs Franklin was still there, and if she was, to remove her. She resented the interest her fiancé's mother was showing in Lucy, just as she had resented Mark's interest in the past.

'Such a pity Camilla felt the need to take on this anaesthetic job,' Mrs Franklin said with a sigh. 'They see so little of each other, even though they're working in the same town.'

'But better than if she'd stayed in London,' Lucy pointed out. 'Mark must have been pleased when she gave up that job at Queen's for his sake.'

'He might have been if it had happened like that,' Mrs Franklin agreed drily. 'Astonished too, I should think.' At Lucy's enquiring look she explained that the job Camilla had wanted had gone to someone else. 'They had an unexpected applicant at the last moment, who was more experienced. Camilla was furious, so she came here as second best. You would have thought——' She broke off, frowning and biting her lip.

Lucy was surprised by her frankness. It was obvious that Mrs Franklin was decidedly critical of her future daughter-in-law's behaviour, possible even that she disliked her, though Camilla had been honey-sweet when she addressed the older woman. 'If I were Mark's mother,' thought Lucy, 'I wouldn't like a girl who played around with my son the way Camilla has done with Mark.'

'You're not really related, are you?' she asked. 'She called you Aunt Beth.'

'A hangover from childhood. My husband and John Fielding had known each other since their schooldays, and Mark and Camilla were more like brother and sister when they were small. Indeed we were astonished——' She paused, as if aware of indiscretion, then went on, speaking more to herself than to Lucy—'We were astonished when they fell in love.' And not altogether pleased, to judge by her rueful expression. She smiled faintly and leant forward to touch Lucy's hand. 'My turn for confidence, dear, but you seem to understand Mark so well. Tell me honestly, do you think they're right for each other?'

Lucy remembered Mark's warning—that his mother could be indiscreet—and felt uneasy. 'I can't possibly say. I—suppose they must be, because they've—they've known each other so long.'

'Too long! They should either have married or have parted, but Camilla wants to have her cake and eat it. Mark *and* a career. Such a pity he couldn't have fallen in love with a sweet, gentle, domesticated type of girl.'

Lucy leant back in her chair and laughed in spite of herself at this idea. 'He'd bully her unmercifully. He needs someone to stand up to him.'

'Yes, you're right.' Mrs Franklin laughed too. 'What a sensible girl you are, Lucy. I told Mark how wrong he'd been about you.'

'Yes, I know and I don't think he believed you.' Her voice was forlorn. 'I wish he had,' she sighed, put a hand to her forehead and rubbed it wearily.

'You're tired, dear,' Mrs Franklin said quickly. 'I've been talking too much.' She had half risen in her chair, when she looked at Lucy and sat down again. 'My dear child——' Her voice was full of concern—'you're crying! What's wrong?' Lucy shook her head and fumbled for a handkerchief, and Mrs Franklin pressed a delicate lace trimmed square into her hand. 'I've been a very foolish woman,' she went on quietly, 'babbling away about my son and Camilla. You care for him, don't you? How stupid of me not to realise it sooner.'

Lucy raised a stricken face to the other woman and made no attempt to deny it. 'Yes, I do,' she said sadly. 'I love him very much. That's why I mind that he thinks badly of me.'

'He has no right to think badly of you,' Mrs Franklin countered with unusual sharpness, 'even if it was true about you and that young man.' She was silent for a moment or two, then she went on slowly, 'I suppose you think me stuffy and old-fashioned, Lucy, but I by no means approve of the way Mark and Camilla behave.'

Lucy didn't pretend to misunderstand her. 'They *are* engaged. Doesn't that make a difference?'

'It most certainly does not!' Mrs Franklin snapped, for the moment very much a product of her background and generation. 'Would *you* sleep with your fiancé before you were married?'

Lucy stared back at her, thought of making some vague rejoinder, but decided to be honest. 'Yes, Mrs Franklin, I expect I would, because if I was engaged to him I'd be in love with him, wouldn't I?'

Mrs Franklin's brows drew together and Lucy was afraid she had gone down in the older woman's estimation. Then suddenly and unexpectedly she smiled. 'My dear child, I admire your honesty. I suppose my generation must learn to adapt.' She rested her chin on her hand and stared out of the window. 'Mark has chosen his way of life, but at times I think he regrets it. However, he's an honourable man, and he has committed himself to Camilla. So he must marry her . . .' Her voice tailed away and she let out a long sigh. 'Mark says I talk too much! I'd better go, my dear, before I become really indiscreet.'

Her farewell kiss on Lucy's cheek was full of affection. 'I shall look in again,' she promised.

After she had gone Lucy lay back in her chair and thought about Mrs Franklin's last remarks. Had she meant that Mark was growing tired of Camilla, that he would have broken off the engagement if he had had the choice? She had said that her son was an honourable man and Lucy knew that was true. Mark might be modern in his life style, but he had old-fashioned ideas about loyalty and commitment. He would not let Camilla down.

'Why, Miss Grant, you're a long way away!' The staff nurse had come into the room without Lucy noticing her. 'Time for a rest, dear. You're looking very tired today.'

The one good thing to come out of Lucy's accident was the change it produced in her father. Already a different man as a result of his psychiatric treatment, Mr Grant rose to the occasion in a way no one would have expected six months ago. He took over the accounts, he did the shopping, he even helped William with the vegetable patch. And that, knowing her father's dislike of gardening, was the surest sign of all that he was getting back to normal.

'I hope you'll be pleased with our efforts,' he remarked on one of his afternoon visits, 'though we haven't done much to the flower beds.'

'Darling Daddy, I'm sure you've had no time!' Lucy exclaimed, laying his hand against her cheek affectionately. 'You've been absolutely marvellous, and so has William.'

'Susan too,' he reminded her. 'She waits on the visitors at table now.'

'She only started doing that when those two students were with us,' William pointed out, 'and then she could hardly stop again, could she?'

Lucy laughed. 'That's unkind, William.'

'But true,' he persisted. 'Girls are so silly, spending all their time thinking about boys. Most girls anyway. You aren't like that, Luce.'

If only he knew, thought Lucy, for she had become nearly as foolish as her young sister. She spent far too much time thinking about Mark. It would be a good thing when she was allowed home, for even if she wasn't able to work for a couple of months, she could do something to help. Being a part of normal family life again would take her mind off her own problems.

Mrs Franklin didn't pay her another visit, for she was called away suddenly by the illness of her sister. Mark came to tell her this a few days later. He arrived when she was eating her lunch, and her hand shook so that she splashed jelly and custard on to her dressing-gown.

'Messy girl!' he exclaimed, handing her a paper tissue from the box by her bed.

Lucy bent her head and rubbed vigorously, while Mark gave her his mother's message. 'She was sorry she couldn't say goodbye. She seems to have taken a great fancy to you.' There was a dry note in his voice and Lucy looked up quickly, to catch an expression on his face that she found difficult to interpret.

'Why, Mark'—she started again—'surely you don't mind that your mother and I have become friendly?'

'I could answer that better if I knew just how friendly,' Mark observed, the dryness even more pronounced. At her blank look he added evenly, 'My mother can be very indiscreet. In plain words she talks too much.' Under his steady gaze Lucy could feel her colour mounting. 'So I was right—she has been gossiping to you, about Camilla and me? Couldn't you have stopped her, Lucy? I did warn you what she was like.'

He rose abruptly and crossed to the window. Lucy stared at his back, the broad shoulders held stiffly, hands thrust into the pockets of his white coat. 'I'm sorry, Mark,' she said unhappily. 'It wasn't easy to stop her, you know.'

'Because you didn't want to,' Mark growled. 'Like all women you adore a good gossip.'

'That's a stupid generalisation,' Lucy snapped back, her own temper beginning to rise now. 'Your mother and I have a lot in common—gardening, music—we're on the same wavelength. If she said more than she should have done——'

'Exactly what did she say?'

'Nothing very terrible.'

'I want to know, Lucy.'

She gave a helpless little shrug. 'She thinks it's about time you and Camilla got married. She worries about you, which is why she was indiscreet. She needed someone to talk to and—and I was available.'

'Yes, of course,' he said disagreeably. 'Little Lucy, the good listener! I've fallen for all that sweet sympathy myself, in the past.'

'Why are you being so nasty, Mark? I've told you I'm sorry.'

He banged his fist down on her small bed table, so that the remains of the jelly shook. 'Oh, God!' he muttered violently. 'If this goes on much longer I shall end up in St Margaret's!'

St Margaret's was their local mental hospital. Lucy eyed him apprehensively. 'Mark, please——'

'Goodbye, Lucy,' he said abruptly, and strode out of the room, banging the door shut after him.

That evening Caroline and Henry came to tell her their news. They were getting married when Caroline finished her present house job, which would be at the beginning of October. Henry had another six months in his present post, so they would live in one of the hospital apartments.

'I've already booked it with the hospital secretary,' Henry said happily. 'He told me we were lucky to get one at such short notice, but I've only just persuaded Caro to make up her mind.'

Lucy smiled warmly at them both. 'I'm so glad! But it is short notice. However are we going to arrange things in time?'

'I don't want a large-scale wedding,' Caroline said firmly, 'and nor does Henry. Just a quiet register office affair, and our closest friends and family at the house afterwards.'

'It sounds a bit ... casual,' Lucy said doubtfully. 'Don't you want a church wedding? And a proper reception?'

But Caroline said they had made up their minds. That sort of wedding was not for them. Her bleep went at that moment, so she went off to the nearest telephone to find out who wanted her. Henry stayed to talk to Lucy, and they gossiped about nothing special for a minute or two. Then Henry looked at her very seriously.

'Lucy——' he hesitated for a moment looking uncomfortable, 'there's something I ought to tell you. I hope it won't upset you, but I feel you ought to know.' He walked up and down the small room, went rather pink and finally sat down beside her. 'People are gossiping,' he said slowly, 'about you and Mark.' Lucy could only gape at him. 'I know,' he nodded, 'it's quite ridiculous, but one of the house physicians saw him rush out of your room this afternoon, apparently very worked up about something. She was talking about it at supper. She said other people had noticed things too—that it was Mark who brought you in when you had your accident, that he'd lived in your house for quite a time—she brought it all up. And the others listened, and added things of their own.'

'And you let them?'

'I did my best to stop them,' Henry said awkwardly, 'but you know how hospitals thrive on gossip. Caro wasn't there or she'd have hit the roof.'

'Have you told her?'

'No. But she'll probably hear about it.'

Other people too. Possibly Camilla, who had an apartment in the hospital, and if she heard about it she would talk to Mark. Lucy shut her eyes and lay quite still.

Henry touched her hand lightly. 'I'm sorry, Lucy. Perhaps I shouldn't have mentioned it.'

She opened her eyes again. 'No, Henry, you were quite right. Why are people so beastly? Who started it?'

'Jane Linton. She hates Mark because he turned her down for his job, and made it quite plain why.'

Jane Linton, the girl who had gossiped about Mark and Lucy in the past. Mark had said he would never employ her and he had kept his word.

'I don't understand,' Lucy sighed. 'You would think a doctor wouldn't be so petty, that a career like medicine would give one a decent set of values.'

Henry laughed rather ruefully. 'You're an idealist, Lucy! There are unpleasant doctors just as there are unpleasant patients. In a way I feel sorry for Jane. She's not a happy girl and she's not popular. That's what makes her so spiteful.'

'Maybe you can be charitable about her, but I'm on the receiving end. She's a thoroughly nasty person and she doesn't deserve to be popular. I'm rather tired, Henry. I think I'll get into bed.'

She lay for a long time, worried and unhappy. It would be dreadful if either Camilla or Mark heard the stories that were going round. It would be unpleasant for Mark as a new consultant, if his reputation was tarnished in any way. She made up her mind to talk her orthopaedic surgeon into letting her go home—at once if possible; by the end of the week at the very latest.

CHAPTER TWELVE

In the end Lucy went home on the last Saturday in September, exactly a month before Caroline's wedding. The orthopaedic surgeon wanted to see her before she left, and wasn't free until the afternoon, so she had to hang about the hospital all morning. When he had pronounced himself satisfied with her, a porter wheeled her over to the residents' house to find Caroline and Henry, who were going to drive her home.

Chris Stevens was waiting for her in the common-room. 'They'll be an hour or so, I'm afraid. Henry's in theatre, anaesthetising for my boss. And Caroline's standing in for one of the other house physicians, who's not well.'

'It doesn't matter,' said Lucy. 'They were going to run me home in the morning, only Dr Carter insisted on seeing me before I left.' She smiled at Chris. 'He threatened me with readmission if I'm not making good progress, when he sees me in Out-patients next week.'

Chris nodded his agreement. 'He's absolutely right, and you must do what he says. Patients often regress when they go home, because they get lazy about their exercises. How often will you be coming to physio?'

'Three times a week. They've fixed up a hospital car, but I wish we still had our own.'

'If I'm free I'll drive you,' Chris said promptly. 'Would you like some tea while you're waiting?'

He would have wheeled her into the dining-room, but Lucy insisted on using her crutches. They were the first people at the big table in the bay window, but within minutes all the seats were taken.

'I didn't realise so many of you were on at weekends,' remarked Lucy, and Chris explained. 'Half on, half off!

And not all the ones who are free go away.'

The talk was mainly medical, in spite of Lucy's presence, but she was used to Caroline and her friends, so she found it amusing and absorbing. They were a friendly bunch, and she was relieved that Jane Linton wasn't one of the young doctors round the table. It would have made her feel uncomfortable if she had had to speak to the girl.

'When are we going to have another musical get-together?' asked the Welshman who had sung with Lucy at the last party.

Lucy smiled. 'Not yet, I'm afraid. I shan't be able to use the foot pedal on the piano for quite a time.'

'Sooner than you think, perhaps,' said Mark from behind her. He rested a hand on her shoulder. 'Ideal physiotherapy, my dear Lucy.'

She stiffened at his touch and cursed herself for the beginning of a blush. 'Hallo, Mark,' she murmured, without turning round. 'I thought you were in Theatre.'

'My registrar's finishing off.' Mark hitched a chair forward from another table and sat down close to Lucy. 'Glad you're going home?'

'Oh yes!' She put all the relief she felt into the words, and his eyebrows went up.

'Was it that awful? I thought we treated you rather well —your own room off the ward, more visitors than most patients are allowed.'

'I know Mark, and I realise I'm lucky to have a sister who's a doctor. But however well you're treated, hospital life begins to drag.'

He smiled disbelievingly. 'All those young doctors? The consultants have been complaining that their lads were skimping their work to visit you!'

Everyone laughed, and Lucy smiled rather self-consciously.

'Can I get you some tea, sir?' asked Chris, and Mark nodded.

'Thanks, Stevens.' He slid into the chair Chris had

vacated, so that he was closer to Lucy. 'Dr Carter tells me you're doing fine. He says the fracture's uniting well and your muscle tone is improving.'

Lucy was touched that he had bothered to enquire about her. She turned quickly towards him, looking properly at him for the first time. He was casually dressed in a black polo-necked sweater. His hair was still damp from the shower that most surgeons seemed to take after an operation and his grey eyes were intent. His expression was concerned, friendly, as if he had forgotten all about their last meeting. Lucy had not, however. She cast a quick glance round, saw that everyone else was involved in other conversations, and took the plunge.

'Mark, I'm glad I've seen you before I go. I should have hated to part on unfriendly terms.'

'Would you, my dear? So you've forgiven me for being so unkind to you?' At her surprised look he added wryly, 'I should never have spoken the way I did.'

'Oh, Mark,' she whispered, 'I was at fault too.'

There was a little pause. 'Nice Lucy,' he said lightly. 'My mother's right, you're a girl in a million!'

Their chairs were so close that their shoulders were touching. Looking up into Mark's tanned and handsome face, Lucy was unconscious of everybody else. She leant closer to him to catch what he was saying, and caught her breath at the way he was looking at her. With affection. With tenderness. With regret?

'Oh, Mark . . .' she murmured, then caught herself up as a clear, spiteful voice came from the next table.

'She has absolutely no pride at all. Just look at her now! If I were Camilla——'

'Oh, shut up, Jane,' a man said gruffly. 'You've done enough damage already.'

Jane Linton's remark might have been missed by most people, except that by an unfortunate chance there had been a temporary lull in the conversation. At the precise moment when she had spoken hardly anyone was talking.

Lucy hadn't noticed the girl sit down at the smaller table to one side of them. She bit her lip and stared unhappily at Mark, praying that he hadn't understood. There was an uncomfortable silence, and she was conscious of the residents around them listening intently.

Chris had returned. 'Your tea, sir.' He put it down clumsily, so that it splashed into the saucer. 'Do you take sugar?'

Mark ignored him. His face was taut, hard, angry. He turned slowly in his chair and stared steadily at Dr Linton. The girl changed colour. She was visibly shaken by the result of her words, which she had certainly not expected Mark to hear. She stretched out a hand for a piece of cake.

Mark spoke, his voice icy. 'Would you explain what you just said, Miss Linton?'

Jane's hand dropped to her side. She gave a silly giggle. 'I was just talking to my friends, Mr Franklin. I didn't expect you to listen.'

'I could hardly fail to hear,' Mark said coldly. 'What did you mean by it?'

'N-nothing really,' stammered the girl, hot-faced and perspiring. She stretched out her hand again for the cake, took a piece and began to crumble it nervously.

Mark went on staring at her, while Chris dropped heavily into the chair someone had vacated. 'Bread and butter, sir? Jam?' He sounded quite desperate, and a young doctor across the table started to laugh, but stopped quickly when Mark glared at him.

'Please don't make a fuss,' Lucy said under her breath. 'Please ignore her,' but Mark had already pushed his chair back.

'I want to talk to you, Miss Linton. Outside.' He hovered over the girl, who now looked thoroughly frightened. She rose reluctantly, close to tears, and Mark clamped a hand on her shoulder.

As they went out together someone whistled. 'My God! I wouldn't care to be in her place!'

'Serve the bitch right! She had it coming.'

People were giving Lucy curious looks, to see how she was taking it. Chris moved up into Mark's seat and put an arm round her shoulders. 'I'm sorry! I'm sorry! What a horrible thing to happen.'

She did her best to put a brave face on it. If she showed how upset she was it would only cause more talk. She longed for Caroline and Henry to come so that she could get away. She hoped that Mark wouldn't return.

In that she was disappointed. He strode back into the room, grim-faced, stalked across to the tea urn and poured himself a fresh cup. The residents studiously avoided looking at him, and started talking among themselves. Mark joined Lucy and Chris without saying anything. He sat stirring his tea and frowning down at his cup, while the silence dragged on. Lucy tried to think of something to say, anything to relieve the tension.

'Was Henry anaesthetising for you?'

Mark didn't answer. Several of the young doctors began to leave, then Lucy saw the ones who were still at the table staring towards the door. She half turned in her chair, wondering what they were looking at.

Camilla had come in. She stood for a moment, gazing around the big room, very erect, her head held high in the familiar manner. Her mouth was compressed and there was a faint colour on her cheeks.

'Oh dear,' sighed Chris, and his hand closed protectively over Lucy's.

There was no doubt that Camilla had heard something. Lucy looked down at her plate and prayed that there was not going to be another scene. After a moment's hesitation Camilla crossed the room and sat down beside them. She looked straight at Mark.

'Hallo, darling. I'm sorry I'm late.' Her gaze travelled to Lucy. 'So you're going home, dear? You must be very pleased.'

The residents, who had fallen silent again, were watching avidly. If they feared (or hoped) for another confrontation, they didn't get it. Camilla behaved beautifully, controlling the conversation, like an expert hostess, steering it firmly into innocuous channels.

Lucy had never liked her, but for the first time she admired her wholeheartedly. There was no question but that Camilla knew what had happened; her expression when she first came into the room had made that plain. However, she had courage and dignity. She would not let her colleagues see if she was upset. She would not demean herself by being unpleasant in public.

'But how she must dislike me,' thought poor Lucy, struggling hard to maintain her composure, and envying Camilla her superior poise. She let out a small sigh of relief when Chris suggested that they should go and wait for Henry and Caroline in the common-room. He helped her to her feet, for she was still a little awkward when she tried to stand up. She fumbled with her crutches, stammered goodbye to Mark and Camilla, and with Chris's arm around her, turned towards the door.

'Go carefully,' Mark said quietly, and Camilla returned Lucy's goodbye rather absently, her eyes on her fiancé. She was still looking at him as they left the room.

Chris blew his cheeks out expressively. 'Phew! I'm glad that's over. I've never liked the woman, but she behaved jolly well, didn't she?'

'Yes, she did,' Lucy agreed. 'Oh, Chris, how could she have heard so quickly?'

'Some busybody who thought she ought to know. It's amazing how some so-called friends rush to tell a person bad news. Or perhaps a genuine friend who wanted her to be prepared.' Chris's arm tightened. 'I'm sorry you had to be there, Lucy. It would have been so much better if Franklin hadn't made a fuss.'

'You think he should have let her get away with it?'

'I think it would have been more tactful to ignore her. Now everyone will think there really is something to it.'

He held open the common-room door, and Lucy was relieved to see that it was empty. She dropped thankfully into a chair, rested her head against its back and stared at the ceiling. 'Mark's not like that, Chris. He believes in having things out in the open.'

'Yes, I know, and I admire him for it in a way. But he ought to have realised how unpleasant it would be for you.'

'It's over now,' Lucy said thankfully, 'so let's try to forget about it. I wish the others would hurry up.'

This unpleasant episode marred Lucy's pleasure in her homecoming a little, but she was touched by the warmth of her reception. Beryl came first, leaping up at her before she was even out of the car, half mad with delight at seeing her again.

The sun was low on the horizon, lighting the mellow old bricks of Marsh House, and waiting in the doorway were her father, Susan and William. Behind them stood Mrs Green, dazzling in a blue and orange apron, and beside her two familiar figures, both grinning broadly— the young Post Office engineers, who had returned for a few days.

Caroline and Henry carried her triumphantly over the threshold and into the sitting-room. Only it wasn't the sitting-room! They had moved Lucy's bed down, so that she wouldn't have to negotiate the stairs.

'We couldn't risk another accident,' Susan explained, and Brian the ebullient winked at Lucy.

'I offered to carry you up and down, but they didn't approve. Nice to see you again, love.'

'And you, Brian. Oh, it's good to be back!' Lucy blinked her eyes hard, feeling absurdly emotional. It wasn't just the pleasure of familiar surroundings, it was the relief from tension, for the scene with Jane Linton had upset her more than she cared to admit.

Mrs Green came to say goodbye. 'It's time I picked up the children—Mum's been looking after them today. Now you're not to worry, Miss Grant, I'll stay as long as I'm needed.'

That was a relief too, and she should have been feeling very happy, but after the first excitement was over she felt curiously flat. They had left her on her own for a while, and she sat in the window staring out at her beloved garden, trying to come to terms with the fact that she would be seeing very little of Mark from now on. In view of the talk about them he was not likely to seek her out, and they had no reason for meeting, so that the most she could hope for was some brief encounter when she was attending physiotherapy. If she had any sense she should be pleased by this state of affairs. It was not pleasant to be talked about as the girl who had come between Mark and his fiancée. If she had any sense—but where Mark was concerned her heart ruled her head, and she longed to see him, however casually.

'Do you approve of Caroline's plans for the wedding?' her father asked, when he brought in her supper on a tray. They had made her go to bed early, because they said she looked fagged out.

'Not really, but it is her day.'

'I should have liked her to get married in our own church —a proper reception, a marquee on the lawn, all the family invited.'

'But they want a quiet wedding Dad, only their favourite relatives and their closest friends. Apart from the expense of a big wedding——'

'So it all comes back to money,' her father frowned. 'If I had a decent job things would have been so different.' He brooded on this less often than he had been used to doing, and he soon cheered up when Lucy started talking about plans for the future.

'I had a lot of time to think in hospital. How about taking caravanners and campers in the field behind the barn? It would boost our income and I'm sure we could get a licence.'

*

Though she was not able to help much in the physical sense Lucy managed to keep quite busy. There were letters to answer from prospective clients, mending to be done and a dozen other small jobs to fill in her days. The garden and the house she had to leave to the others, for Dr Carter was insistent that she must not yet let weight bear on her injured leg.

She never met Mark on her trips to the hospital, and the day of the wedding was rapidly approaching. Would he come? Had they invited him? Casually she asked to see the list of guests.

Caroline, who was home for the evening, smiled and said that there wasn't one. 'We know roughly who's coming. About a dozen relatives, and perhaps twenty from the hospital.'

'Is Mark one of them?' asked Lucy.

'He's on call that day. I suppose he could have got away if he'd really wanted to, but it's not as if we're old friends.'

'No, of course not,' Lucy agreed with a little sigh, and Henry added that Mark was very edgy these days. Everyone was commenting on it.

'I expect it's because Camilla has gone,' said Caroline, and Lucy jumped in quickly.

'Gone? Gone where?'

'How should I know? Finished her locum, been offered something better. Or perhaps she was fed up over that silly talk about you and Mark.'

'Perhaps she's taking time off to organise her own wedding,' suggested Lucy, relieved to find she could speak the words quite calmly.

'Yes, I expect that's it. I expect they want to squash the rumours as soon as possible.'

Everything went right for Caroline on her great day. They rose to a thick autumn mist, which cleared by eleven to leave dazzling sunshine. When they left the register office in Barnslow the ambulance men, who had their headquarters next door, turned out en masse to cheer the young doctors, and Lucy, following behind on her crutches, was touched by this evidence of medical camaraderie. There was so much in the newspapers about the bad relations between different sectors of the Health Service, but there wasn't much evidence of it in Barnslow.

'Hallo, love! Remember us?' The two ambulance men who had been called to the orchard on the day of her accident were waving and smiling at her.

When the wedding party arrived back at Marsh House, Lucy fretted because she couldn't do more.

'You sit and look decorative,' Henry told her, then brought his parents over to keep her company and returned to his bride.

Caroline was looking almost beautiful, her thin face radiant, her pale cheeks becomingly flushed. She wore an ankle-length dress, the colour of clotted cream, ruched and tucked so that her slight figure appeared more rounded than usual. She looked what she was, a young woman deeply in love, and although Lucy was sincerely happy for her, she felt a small pang of envy. Her own future looked so bleak. Years of hard work running the house, until Susan and William grew up and left home. They might move to a smaller house after that, but it would be too late to return to her musical career, and the prospect of falling in love again seemed as remote as a trip to the moon—an unlikely event, though she tried to tell herself it did happen. It could happen to her.

'Are you all right, dear?' Henry's mother asked, jolting her out of these gloomy thoughts.

'I'm a little tired, Mrs Wilson.' There was always the excuse of her accident if she seemed less cheerful than everyone else.

She used the same excuse later, when Henry and Caroline had driven off to London, to catch a night plane to Greece, where they were spending their honeymoon. She didn't feel up to a long family session, and even less like a post-

wedding celebration with the hospital residents, who tried
to talk her into going back with them.

'I wish you would,' said Susan, 'then I could go too.'

She looked deliciously pretty in a dress of broderie an-
glaise threaded through with blue ribbon, and Lucy had
noted with amusement that Chris could hardly take his
eyes off her. It would be an excellent thing if he diverted
his attention to her young sister, for Lucy knew that she
could never feel more for him than liking.

'You can go without me,' she smiled, and Susan brightened.

Mr Grant was inclined to object, saying Susan was too
young for an adult party. 'Especially a medical party,' he
frowned, unexpectedly the heavy father.

Lucy laughed him out of it. 'You do have a low opinion
of Caro's profession, Dad! They're not medical students
still. They've grown up.'

'That's just it,' said her father. 'Susan hasn't.'

'But Chris will look after her, see she doesn't do anything
silly. Please let her go, Dad.'

He gave way reluctantly, and as the young doctors departed he studied his second daughter curiously. 'I thought
Chris was your young man, Lucy? Don't you mind that
he seems to have transferred his interest?'

When she smiled and shook her head, he put an arm
around her shoulders and hugged her. 'My dearest child,
you ought to have someone of your own. You're young
and pretty, but you act like a middle-aged spinster.'

'I'm waiting for Mr Right!' said Lucy, making a joke of
it to divert his attention, and was relieved when her Aunt
Mary came over to join them.

Her aunt and uncle were staying the night, though the
rest of the visitors had left by seven. Lucy went to bed
early, and after a bad night overslept, a rare thing for her.
She was horrified to see the time when Susan brought in a
cup of tea and announced that Uncle Bill and Aunt Mary
would soon be off.

'Oh, goodness, I'm sorry!' Lucy exclaimed, sitting up and sipping rapidly.

'It's O.K.,' said young Susan. 'Why shouldn't you sleep in? Last night was super, Luce!' She plonked herself on the end of the bed, looking dreamy and dewy-eyed. 'You don't really care about Chris, do you?' she asked anxiously, and when Lucy said she didn't Susan looked very relieved. 'Because I like him a lot, and—and I think he likes me.' She looked young and unsure of herself, and Lucy felt a moment's unease. However, Susan would be seventeen shortly. She was growing up fast, and Chris was reliable. He would not take advantage of her inexperience.

Lucy dressed as quickly as she could, though she was still rather clumsy, and went to join the family. Aunt Mary was urging William to work hard at school, an unnecessary injunction which was making him look increasingly irritated.

'Silly old cow,' he muttered as the dark blue Rover drew out of the yard.

'She means well,' Lucy said charitably. 'Help me along to the seat by the pond, William.' She found the uneven ground difficult to negotiate on her own and was frightened of another fall.

Her brother guided her to the wooden seat by the little pond. 'Do you want a paper, Lucy? Or a book or anything?'

'No, dear, I'll just sit for a time.'

'Girls are so weird,' he said pityingly. 'I couldn't just sit.'

Smiling, Lucy watched his thin young figure disappear round the corner of the shrubbery. Once she would have echoed his opinion; she had not been a great one for sitting and thinking herself. Now she found great solace in the garden after five weeks of being shut up in a hospital ward.

The day was warm for October, with not a trace of wind. The pond was pleasant to look at, with the red water-

lilies still in bloom and the goldfish darting in and out
among the plants. Her father's words came back to her
mind. Was she becoming an old maid? A ridiculous idea!
She was only twenty-two and reasonably pretty. She would
go out with young men if they asked her, try to lead a
normal life again. She would not let a hopeless love spoil
her whole life. She rested her chin on one hand and stared
down at the pond, deep in thought, so that she didn't hear
footsteps approaching along the flagged path.

'Hallo, Lucy!' She jerked her head up, to find Mark
standing on the opposite side of the small pool, watching
her steadily.

She had been thinking about him a moment before, but
she was so dazed by his sudden appearance that she was
incapable of saying anything. Mark's smile slipped a little.
He shoved his hands into his pockets and dug a heel into a
clump of michaelmas daisies.

'Don't do that,' Lucy said quickly. 'I've been trying to
grow them for ages.'

He looked down, removed his heel and said he was sorry.

'I thought you were on duty this weekend,' she went on,
and he shook his head.

'I was standing in for one of the other surgeons yesterday
afternoon. It was a pity it coincided with Caroline's wedding, but I'd promised before I knew the date.'

'You mean you'd have come if you hadn't been working?'

He looked surprised at her question. 'Of course, my dear
girl. You were the first friends I made when I came to
Barnslow.'

'Oh, Mark! That's kind of you, considering what the set-
up really was.'

'Don't be silly, Lucy.' He made no move to join her,
though there was room on the seat. He looked very handsome with the sunshine gleaming on the top of his thick
dark hair. Handsome and unattainable.

'Why have you come, Mark?' she asked jerkily, and
regretted that at once. Hadn't he just said they were his

oldest friends? Why shouldn't he visit them? Then another thought struck her.

'Did Camilla come too?' she asked. He said nothing for a moment. 'Is she with the others, Mark?'

He walked round the pond then, and sat down beside her. 'Camilla and I have broken up,' he said quietly. 'We're no longer engaged.'

Lucy thought she knew now why he had come—for sympathy, to let off steam. He had said in the past that she was a good listener.

'Oh, Mark, I'm so sorry.' She loved him enough to want his happiness, even if it went against her own.

'I'm not,' Mark said sharply, and when she stared at him, 'Not sorry, Lucy.' He spoke brusquely, biting off the words almost before he had said them. He gave her one of his direct looks and her heart began to beat faster at the expression on his face. 'I've longed for her to break off our engagement for weeks—for months even.'

'But . . . why?' It came out as a whisper.

'You know why. Don't pretend.'

There was a tightness in Lucy's chest, a roaring in her ears. The sunshine was too bright. 'Lucy!' Mark seemed to be speaking from a long way away. 'What's wrong? You're upset. I thought, after what Mother told me, that you'd be pleased.'

He caught her by the shoulders and drew her against him, and she rested her head against his chest, trying to believe that it was really happening. 'I love you, Lucy,' Mark went on. 'I've known since that awful day when you fell out of the tree. I think I really knew it before that, only I wouldn't admit it because of Camilla.'

Camilla! Lucy stirred uneasily. 'Mark, is she very unhappy about it? When did you tell her?'

'On the day you left hospital. She brought it up herself, asked me directly, was I in love with you. When I said yes, she didn't seem very surprised.'

'But . . . wasn't she terribly unhappy?' It would dim her

own joy if she was the cause of another girl's heartache.

'I think she was really rather relieved.' Mark's smile was wry. 'Our engagement was a mistake, we can both see that now. She's applying for an overseas job with the World Health Organisation, and I'm sure she'll get it. Camilla's a career woman at heart.'

And yet ... and yet she *had* resented Lucy. Possessiveness rather than love? A common enough human failing, and Camilla had more than her share of faults, though she also possessed good qualities—dedication to her work, dignity, courage.

'I didn't used to like her,' Lucy said slowly, 'but I've changed my mind,' and conscious that that sounded odd, she added quickly, 'Not just because she's let you go. She was marvellous over that unpleasant scene with Dr Linton.'

Mark had had enough of discussing his past love affair. 'When are you going to marry me, darling?'

Her heart was in her eyes as she looked at him. 'As soon as I can walk properly. You wouldn't want a bride on crutches!'

They clung together then, laughing and happy. Mark sobered first and put her gently away from him. 'You do realise, my love, that there'll be a good deal of gossip at the hospital?'

'I don't care,' Lucy said stoutly.

'Of course it will only be a nine days' wonder, but it could be unpleasant while it lasts.'

'I don't care,' Lucy repeated, then wondered a shade uneasily what Caroline would say. Her momentary uneasiness was swept away by Mark's next words.

'Come on then, let's tell your family now.' He picked her up and strode off down the path.

'Mark, my crutches! I can't manage without them. I'm not supposed to stand yet.'

'You don't have to,' Mark retorted. 'I'll support you,' so with a contented sigh Lucy relaxed in his arms.

William was tinkering with a transistor on the small lawn

in front of the house. When he saw Lucy in Mark's arms he jumped to his feet in alarm. 'What's happened? Has she hurt herself again?'

'No, William.' Mark put her down carefully on the low brick wall, and smiled at his future brother-in-law. 'Lucy and I are going to get married, and you're the first to know.'

William's freckled face was puzzled, then disapproving. 'I don't think that's very funny,' he said gruffly. 'You're engaged to Camilla.'

'Not any more. I'm engaged to your sister now.'

A slow flush spread over the boy's face. He cast an appealing look at Lucy, his embarrassment and confusion all too plain.

'It's true, William. Mark and Camilla decided they didn't want to get married after all.'

'Oh!' Still William looked unhappy, as if the vagaries of adults were quite beyond him.

'You'll get used to the idea,' Mark said kindly, less put out than Lucy was by the boy's reaction. 'Go and tell the others we've some news for them.' As William darted off with obvious relief, he sat down on the wall beside Lucy. 'Don't look so upset. It was quite a shock to the lad. There's another problem we have to face—where we're going to live.'

'But what's wrong with your house?'

'The house is fine, and the builders have finished at last. Only I thought you might not want to live there, because I bought it for Camilla.'

Lucy loved the old house and its beautiful garden. She could see their children growing up there. She could even imagine Mark and herself growing old in it. 'It was never Camilla's,' she said quietly, 'because she took no interest. But would you really have sold it, if that had been what I wanted?'

'My darling girl,' said Mark, slipping an arm round her shoulders and drawing her close, 'I would have sold it without hesitation if you'd asked me.'

She relaxed against him, contented and at peace, until a sudden thought struck her and she drew away from him. How could she have been so selfish, so wrapped up in her own affairs? 'Oh, darling, we can't get married as soon as I'd have liked. I have to look after the house. It's our only source of income.'

'Rubbish! They're managing perfectly well without you.'

'But, Mark——'

'I am not going to get involved in a domestic argument on the first day of our engagement,' Mark said firmly. 'No one's indispensable. You couldn't have been much older than Susan when you took over the running of this place. Let her cope for a change, with Mrs Green to help her. And your father, and William. They're not as helpless as you seem to think, and you won't be far away.'

She looked at him doubtfully. 'Here come your family,' he went on, a thread of amusement in his voice. 'Let's hope they take the news better than William did. My God, the boy's already told them!' for Susan and her father were advancing towards them quickly, watched by William from the front door.

They looked astonished, excited, but not at all disapproving. Indeed as Mark stood up to greet them, Susan gave a delighted giggle, while Mr Grant smiled and gripped the younger man by the hand.

'My dear boy—my dear Lucy ...' Then he ran out of words, and Susan took over.

While her little sister chattered on excitedly, Lucy exchanged a long look with her father. It was going to be all right. Everybody would react to their news with surprise, and some with disapproval, but the people who loved them, the people who were their friends, would understand. The rest didn't matter. Secure in Mark's love, Lucy felt armoured against the world.

What the press says about Harlequin romance fiction...

"When it comes to romantic novels...
Harlequin is the indisputable king."
—*New York Times*

"...exciting escapism, easy reading, interesting
characters and, always, a happy ending....
They are hard to put down."
— *Transcript-Telegram*, Holyoke (Mass.)

"...always...an upbeat, happy ending."
—*San Francisco Chronicle*

"...a work of art."
— *Globe & Mail*, Toronto

"Nothing quite like it has happened since
Gone With the Wind..."
—*Los Angeles Times*